NOW YOU
LOVE ME

Also by Liesel Litzenburger

THE WIDOWER

LIESEL LITZENBURGER

NOW YOU LOVE ME

THREE RIVERS PRESS

NEW YORK

Copyright © 2006 by Liesel Litzenburger

Published in the United States by Three Rivers Press, an imprint of the
Crown Publishing Group, a division of Random House, Inc., New York.
www.crownpublishing.com

Originally published in slightly different form in the United States by
Carnegie-Mellon University Press, Pittsburgh, Pennsylvania, in 2001.

Three Rivers Press is a registered trademark and the Three Rivers Press
colophon is a trademark of Random House, Inc.

These stories appeared (in slightly different forms) in the following
publications: "Pictures from My Father's Trip" in *Michigan Quarterly Review*;
"Porcupines" (under the title "My Inheritance") in *Alaska Quarterly Review*;
and "Now You Love Me" in *Passages North*.

Library of Congress Cataloging-in-Publication Data
Litzenburger, Liesel.
Now you love me / by Liesel Litzenburger.—1st ed.
1. Single mothers—Michigan—Fiction.   2. Love stories, American.
I. Title.
PS3612.I89N69   2007
813'.6—dc22   2006018593

ISBN 978-0-307-33955-3

Printed in the United States of America

Design by Lynne Amft

10   9   8   7   6   5   4   3   2   1

First Edition

This is for my mother,
CAMERON REYCRAFT O'KEEFE,
with love,
for the gift of dreaming.

Contents

NOW YOU
LOVE ME

POINT HARBOR, MICHIGAN

1976

PICTURES FROM MY
FATHER'S TRIP

After I saw the man who could bend spoons with his eyes, everything just fell into place. For a long time, I had known things weren't right, but I didn't exactly know why they were wrong. It wasn't as if I was really looking for the answer to some big question in particular; I was nine. But when I saw the incredible melting of those spoons, even if it was only TV, and heard the man talk about his life as an alien on Earth, I knew that I had some sort of answer even if I wasn't ready for it. The truth of it all just knocked me flat.

It was exactly like the time I fell off the monkey bars and landed smack on my back on the hard-packed dirt. I couldn't breathe for two whole minutes, and in the time it took Miss Baker, who was on playground patrol, and the other kids to notice me lying there, I felt my whole life get sucked right up and disappear into the sky. I was alive, but I was suddenly pulled apart from everyone else, and the sound of the other kids running and screaming and leaping off the slide was like some song that I could hum but didn't really know the words for. Everything looked the same, but completely new, too, and staring up at the gray November sun through the lattice of the monkey bars, I knew somehow that things would never be familiar again. It was like that when I saw the man who could bend spoons; he was so strange that I knew right away how absolutely familiar he truly was.

It was fate or something more that I even saw the spoon-bending business to begin with. I wasn't supposed to be up late enough to see things like that on TV, but my mother was at the country club Christmas party that night with my aunt Claire. Ever since my father had gone away, my aunt Claire tried to get my mother to go out and do things, even offering to help her find a really good babysitter. Our usual babysitter, Grace Nanagost, wasn't one for rules. She let my brother, Gus, and me do mostly whatever we wanted as long as we were quiet and we let her make unlimited blender drinks and try on our mother's clothes. It was a mistake to ask Grace to do anything like play tag in the basement or draw pictures. Like most adults, she liked to be left alone.

The night of the spoon bending, Grace was drinking frothy margaritas, one after the next, and wearing my mother's mink coat around the house. She made the margaritas with the tequila my mother had gotten once in Mexico, refilling the bottle with water each time before she put it back in the liquor cabinet.

"Why don't you go outside and play or something?" she'd ask Gus and me as she paraded through the living room on one of her trips to get a new outfit or mix another drink. "You kids watch too much TV."

Gus and I were sitting on the floor, watching a movie about a man who used kung fu to get his girlfriend back.

"It's dark out," Gus said, playing with a squashed lime rind that Grace had dropped on the floor as she sashayed past.

"Aren't you hot in that coat?" I asked.

"That's the thing about mink," Grace said, taking a swig of her margarita and settling on the couch. "It's an all-weather fur—indoors or out."

"How would you know?" Gus asked. "That's not even your coat."

"I *know* mink," Grace snapped. "I've killed them with my bare hands!"

Grace made a twisting motion like she was wringing out a wet dishcloth. "Like so," she said. She drained her glass and then stretched out flat on the couch, pulling the mink up around her face.

"Oh," Gus said, and looked down at the carpet.

He was five. He believed whatever Grace said. I knew that she was a lot of talk. She wasn't much of a babysitter, either, but we lived in a small town. It was really only much of a town during the summer tourist season when people came to stare at Lake Michigan and buy fake Indian crafts. Babysitters were scarce in the winter, good ones and bad.

"Annie, this is a damn hard couch," Grace snorted from inside the mink. She reached out and turned off the lamp on the table beside her. "I'd think that your mother could afford a whole lot more comfortable couch than this."

"It's chintz," I told her.

I wasn't sure what that meant, it was just something I had heard my mother say, but by that time Grace was snoring anyway.

"Let's turn the sound off and then make up our own words," I said to Gus.

I couldn't understand most of what the kung-fu men were saying, anyway, and I wanted to make him forget about the dead mink.

We turned off the sound and watched the men silently swinging their arms around and kicking each other in the head.

"Ouch," Gus would say once in a while. "Ouch, that hurts."

"No, you have to make up real words," I said. "Stuff like, 'Give me my girlfriend back now, mister, or I'll be forced to kill you!' "

"Oh," Gus said, but then he didn't say anything else and curled up in a ball on the floor and fell asleep or at least pretended to sleep. I thought he was probably just copying Grace.

I watched the rest of the movie and then the news, all with the sound off. By then it was way past my bedtime, but Grace was still snoring from inside my mother's fur coat and Gus was still asleep, too. When the late-night talk show started, I turned the sound up a tiny bit and moved closer so that my face was almost touching the screen. It was better that way. With the room almost completely dark, lit only by the television's watery blue glow, I forgot that anyone else was even there. I knew that my mother wouldn't be home until very late, and since Grace and Gus were asleep, they didn't really count. I felt like the only living being left on the planet, and that made it all the more incredible when the man appeared.

The talk-show host had been interviewing some movie star and then the man came on. With my face that close to the screen, the man's eyes were as big as cereal bowls, and when he spoke, it was like he was whispering right into my ear.

"So you're going to be bending some spoons for us tonight," the talk-show host said.

"I think so," the man said. "That's what I had planned to do."

I studied the man's face. He was very pale and skinny. He looked like he probably watched a lot of TV, too.

"Fabulous," the host said. "Now, you don't use ordinary means to bend these spoons, is that right?"

"Well, not ordinary in *your* sense of the word."

"*My* sense?" the talk-show host asked. He laughed a little, but it sounded fake.

"You, as in an earthling's sense of the word. Where I'm from, it's perfectly normal to be able to bend objects using con-centrated visual energy," the man said.

He sounded bored, like he'd explained the whole thing a million times.

"Oh, I see," the host said. "And where exactly are you from?"

"Another planet, not even in this galaxy, so I won't bother naming it," the man snapped.

"Well, you can see how that would be a bit difficult for some people to believe, can't you?"

"I suppose so," the man said. "But I was raised here on Earth, so you might say that I'm versed in Earth ways as well as those of my home planet. I arrived here as a young boy and was taken in by my Earth family, who raised me as their own, and to them I am truly grateful."

"How did you *arrive* here?" the host asked.

"I was deposited in my Earth family's backyard." The man crossed his arms and gave the host a long stare.

"Well, we're running short on time," the host said, "so without further ado, let's see some spoon bending!"

As the man stood up to prepare to bend the spoons, I sank back to the floor. There was a strange rushing noise in my head, and the whole room seemed to swirl in the darkness around me. It was like I knew what was going to happen next, like I had known it all along. I knew in my heart that I had been deposited, too—that I had the wrong family, the wrong house, and probably the wrong planet. For a second, I felt like I couldn't breathe.

I pressed my face closer to the screen. The man was holding a soupspoon at arm's length and clutching his forehead in the palm of his free hand. The camera zoomed in on his ferocious eyes first and then back to the soupspoon. It made me dizzy the way the camera kept switching back and forth, back and forth. I wanted to see his eyes actually bending the spoon, the whole thing in one shot, but it was like all that power was just too big to fit into one small square of a TV screen.

Finally, as beads of sweat started popping out all over the man's forehead, the spoon suddenly bent and hung limply, as if exhausted, over his sweaty fist. The man held the limp spoon above his head and the audience cheered.

He bent a sterling silver teaspoon next, dabbing his brow with a handkerchief and banging the spoon on a table to prove that it was solid before he began. He clutched his forehead, and the camera flashed to the spoon in giant close-up as it began to shrink away from the man's terrible staring. The spoon caught the light as it bent in an arc around the man's hand, and for a second it looked like a shooting star, like something so beautiful and bright that you know it's an accident you're even seeing it in the first place. I looked away from the screen because it was all too much, and when I looked back, the spoon was twisted in a perfect circle around the man's hand, and the yelling and clapping of the audience was a humming inside my head.

I turned the TV off then and just sat in the dark listening to Grace snoring. I woke Gus and guided him up to his bedroom and made him lie down on his bed. I started to go to my room, but something made me keep walking. I just kept thinking about those spoons and how my even being on Earth could be some kind of mistake. I pushed open the door to my mother's room and went inside. The air was still and warm, like bathwater that's been sitting too long, and I felt like a trespasser just being there. Everything looked so different in the dark: the chair crouched by the window, the silvery mirror above her chest of drawers. Her jewelry was spread out across the dressing table, and when I ran my hand lightly across it, it was like feeling the surface of one of those maps that have real bumps for the mountains, little pockets for the valleys and lakes.

I opened the closet and stared at her clothes. With only the light from the moon coming through the window, it was hard to guess what color everything really was. I thought about Grace downstairs on the couch, wrapped in my mother's coat. I knew what it was like to want to be someone else, even just to pretend.

I sat on the floor of the closet and buried my face in the skirt hems and the dangling sleeves. It all smelled like my mother's perfume and laundry soap and dust, too. I felt around on the floor, touching her shoes and slippers that were all jumbled in one big heap. I reached over into the corner and my hand slipped across something that was set apart from all the other shoes. I could tell right away that whatever it was, it was black. It was like I could feel the exact color with my fingers. I picked it up and held it right in front of my face, breathing in old leather and wax. It was one of my father's wingtips; the right foot, I think. I felt around for the other one, but there was nothing else there.

I remembered my mother boxing up all of my father's clothing and sending it away somewhere. My mother had said that my father was on a trip and that he would be gone for a while. It truly *had* started as a trip; my father had gotten on a plane just to go somewhere. But then he never came back. It got to be like a story we told each other—my father's trip—something we could repeat over and over until it was real. We all knew he was probably gone for good, but I went on pretending to believe about the trip because it was easier that way. I held the shoe tight to my chest and wondered if it was an accident that it was left behind or if my mother had kept it for a reason. I clutched the shoe tighter and thought about my father, what he had done with just one shoe, if he had even noticed that the other was gone. It made me so lonely to think of it, sitting in the closet with that old shoe. But it was more homesickness than anything else. I was just missing my other planet.

The next morning at breakfast I concentrated for a long time, trying to make my cereal spoon do something. I made my eyes into little slits and thought about forest fires and electric blankets and the hottest things that I could imagine, but still nothing happened.

"Annie, what are you doing?" my mother asked, peering at me over the top of her coffee cup.

She was in a bad mood because she had come home to find Grace, smelling like tequila, asleep on the couch in her mink coat. Grace had gone too far. My mother had had to fire Grace on the spot, and now she would have to find a new babysitter.

"Nothing," I said.

I didn't want to tell her about the spoons. She had enough to worry about.

"Well, stop it," my mother said. "You're going to make your eyes cross permanently if you keep doing that."

"Yeah, stop it," Gus chimed in from across the table, but then he picked up his spoon and started staring it down.

"Stop it," my mother said. "Both of you. Go outside and play."

"It's cold out," Gus said.

"It's good for you," my mother said, taking another sip of her coffee. "No TV today. I mean it."

Since it was Saturday, that meant no *Wild Kingdom,* my favorite show. I decided it would be best to go outside right away and then my mother would have forgotten her threat, anyway. She always did. Since my father left it was like she was just too tired to make sure we followed rules.

"Come on, Gus," I said.

We set down our spoons and went to get our hats and coats out of the hall closet.

"Mom's mad," Gus said, wrapping his scarf halfway up his face.

"She's just tired." I suddenly remembered my father's wing-tip under my bed, where I had hidden it the night before. My mother always changed our sheets on Saturday, and I thought about her finding the shoe by accident if she reached under the bed to dust or to straighten the rug. I pictured how she would jerk back in shock if her hand happened to touch it.

"I have to go get something. Just wait here a second."

I ran upstairs to my room and grabbed the shoe from underneath the bed. Just then, I heard my mother coming up the stairs so I pushed the shoe back under and sat up straight.

"Stay close by," my mother said, stopping in the doorway. "And keep an eye on Gus."

"I had to come back up to get my hat." I thought she probably somehow knew exactly what I was up to, that at any second she would ask if I had been in her closet. "I forgot my hat so I had to come back up here to get it."

"Okay," my mother said. "If you get too cold, come back inside."

She walked into her room and shut the door.

I had no choice; I had to take the shoe with me. It was too late to put it back in her closet, and she might find it anyplace else. I unzipped my jacket and stuffed the shoe down my front. I zipped the jacket back over it, but the whole thing wouldn't fit so I had to leave the toe poking out a little bit. It looked like the shiny black nose of some animal I was trying to keep warm.

"You look fat," Gus said as I came down the stairs.

"Shut up," I hissed, pulling him outside.

"You have to help me with something. I have to hide this for a little while," I said, unzipping my jacket slightly to expose more of the shoe.

"Oh." Gus poked at the wingtip with his mittened hand. "Why?"

"Just because," I said, my breath coming out in little puffs.

"We could bury it," Gus offered.

"There's too much snow," I said, surveying the yard, a blanket of white sloping down to the lake.

I started trudging through the snow, heading away from the house. I was afraid that my mother might happen to look out the window and see the shoe poking out of my jacket.

"We could build a giant snowman and use it like it's a foot," Gus puffed after me.

"No," I said. "Everyone could see it that way."

Gus and I circled around the house and came out on our street. No cars had passed yet and the snow was smooth and unbroken. Our boots made little crunching noises.

"We could . . . ," Gus began.

"Be quiet," I said. "I have to think about this."

We were halfway down the street by that time, far enough away so that even if my mother did look out the window, we would look like tiny specks. There was no one else to see us either because there were only six houses on our street and, of those, only ours wasn't boarded up for the winter. The other people who lived on our street were there only in the summer.

I unzipped my jacket all the way and pulled out the shoe. It had been getting heavy, and when I pulled off my mittens and touched the skin under my shirt, I could trace the impression of a half-moon where the heel had been pressing.

"This is Dad's shoe," I told Gus, holding it out so he could see the whole thing. "We have to put it somewhere safe."

"Where did you get it?" Gus asked. "Did Mom give it to you?"

He wiped his nose with the back of his mitten and coughed.

"Not exactly," I said. "I'm just sort of borrowing it for a while."

We waded through the snow and sat on the edge of the Slocums' big white porch. Mr. and Mrs. Slocum were in Florida for the winter. They had boarded up their windows with pieces of plywood painted dark green to match the house's trim, as if they wanted everything to match even when they weren't there. Every year for Christmas, the Slocums sent us a big box of oranges marked "Sunshine from the Sunshine State." Mr. Slocum had a glass eye that moved around in all different directions when he talked.

"Do you have the other shoe, too?" Gus asked, swinging his legs over the edge of the porch.

"I guess Dad has the other one," I said.

"Oh," Gus said. He just kept swinging his legs and was quiet for a while.

"Maybe Dad will remember where he left his other shoe and he'll come back and get it when he's done with his trip, right?" Gus asked.

"Maybe," I said, even though I knew he wouldn't come all the way back for a shoe.

"I know!" Gus said. "Let's put it in the Slocums' mailbox."

Even though Gus was usually bad with ideas, the mailbox really was the perfect place. The mailman never stopped at the Slocums' house in the winter and the mailbox was dry and the perfect size. Gus and I trudged over to the mailbox, painted with mallard ducks on one side and the name SLOCUM in big capital letters on the other. We opened it and stuffed the shoe inside.

"That way," Gus said, "we'll know exactly where it is all the time."

"But you can't tell anyone," I said. "Not Mom or anybody, okay?"

"Okay, I promise."

Before we shut the mailbox door, Gus reached inside and patted the shoe on the toe.

"Good night!" he shouted into the mailbox. The words echoed and sounded deeper than his real voice, as if someone else was calling them out from far away. "Good night; sleep tight!"

For several mornings after that, as we drove by the Slocums' mailbox on our way to school, I would lower my eyes and turn my head just enough to see it. I thought about the shoe a lot, even though Gus seemed to have completely forgotten it. I wondered how cold it was in the mailbox and if shoes could freeze. I wanted to bring it back in the house, but it seemed like my mother was always home. I was afraid that she might discover that the shoe wasn't in her closet and I wondered how mad she would be. I had to look quick to see the mailbox at all because I didn't want my mother to notice me doing it. She was usually thinking of other things, anyway, mostly my new fascination with silverware, I guessed, from the way she gave me worried looks all the time. I was still trying to bend things—spoons, knives, and once in a while a fork or two—and she had threatened to take me to see the doctor if I kept it up. She thought it was some sort of a "compulsion" like the ones she read about in *Vogue* or one of her other magazines.

I had decided to limit my spoon bending to lunchtime so she wouldn't worry so much, but the school cafeteria spoons were so flimsy to begin with, it really wasn't much of a challenge. Besides, I didn't like to call attention to my secret background, and if the other kids saw me trying to bend spoons, they would have asked a lot of stupid questions. They asked stupid questions even without seeing me bend spoons.

"Where is your father, anyway?" Jennifer Peshawbi asked me one day at lunch.

I could tell from the way her voice sounded friendly, but fake, too, that she already knew the answer.

"He's on a trip." I pretended to be really interested in my peanut butter cookie.

"He's sure been on that trip a long time," Jennifer said, fake smiling as she played with one of her long black braids.

"It's a business trip."

"Oh," Jennifer said, but I could tell she didn't believe me.

On the way home from school that afternoon, I told my mother what Jennifer had said.

"Everybody knows. I'm not going to school anymore. I mean it."

"Yeah," Gus chimed in from the backseat. "I *mean* it."

"Shut up!" I yelled.

"Stop it, you two," my mother said in a tired voice. "No fighting."

When we passed the Slocums' mailbox, I noticed that all the new snow had piled up to cover it completely. I imagined the shoe inside, encased in a solid block of ice like when something gets frozen in the cartoons. After we pulled into our driveway and my mother had turned off the car, she started to say something and then stopped and took a big gulp of air instead.

Later, when Gus and I were arguing in the kitchen about who got to eat the last Space Stick, my mother called to us from the living room.

"Come in here a minute," she said. "I have to talk to both of you about something."

I could tell by her voice that it was something bad. Gus followed me into the living room and we sat on the couch next to my mother. She was holding two postcards and she handed one to each of us.

"These came last week," she said, then stopped and took a breath.

I studied the front of my postcard. It was a picture of some mountains. It looked like Switzerland or that huge mountain that all those people have died trying to climb. Gus's had palm trees and a long sandy beach on it. I turned the postcard over and started reading the back.

"Dear Annie," it began. I suddenly didn't want to read any more.

"I was going to just keep them, but then I decided . . . Oh, I don't know." My mother took another deep breath like she was going to cry. "I just decided . . . they're yours, really. Your father meant for you to have them."

"Look!" Gus shouted, waving his postcard in the air. "A picture of Dad's trip!"

"Dear Annie," I read again. "I miss you very much and I wish . . ."

I couldn't read any more than that.

Gus was skipping around the room yelling, "This is a picture of Dad's trip!" and my mother was sitting quietly like if she moved at all she might break apart.

I turned the postcard over and stared at the mountains again. I knew that it wasn't a picture from my father's trip at all, that it could be a picture from anyone's trip, anywhere.

"Dear Annie," I whispered to myself, and then I wished that I could be like Gus and just believe.

That night, I lay in my bed and waited until I was certain that Gus and my mother were asleep. I watched for the light to go off in my mother's room down the hall, and then I waited some more to be sure that she wasn't still awake. I crept downstairs in my nightgown and sat on the floor in the dark, putting on my boots and coat. I quietly unlocked the front door and slipped outside, feeling like a spy on some sort of secret mission. As I started running, freezing air burned my lungs and the snow crackled under my boots like pine needles thrown on a roaring fire. My nightgown kept getting twisted around my legs, but I just couldn't slow down.

When I finally got to the Slocums' mailbox, I realized that I hadn't even worn my mittens, so I had to dig through the snow with my bare hands. I dug with my nails, scratching and raking the crusted snow. By the time I got down to the mailbox's door, my hands felt like they weren't even part of my body.

The shoe looked exactly the same; it didn't even have any frost on it. It scared me somehow to see it sitting there, so silent and black. I grabbed it in one numb hand and started running back toward the house, fast, as if someone were chasing me. That's when my nightgown got caught in the top of one of my boots and I lost my balance and fell backward into a snowbank. The shoe flew out of my hand and I heard it bounce once and go skittering off down the road. I lay still for a second, my whole body stretched out in the snow, every inch of me touching the freezing earth. I stared up at the sky, at the millions of stars pressing down through the darkness. Not one of them had the familiar glow of my own lost planet.

THE DAY BEFORE EASTER

At the Laundromat, a man with no shirt on asked our mother if she wanted to go to the circus with him. First he asked if she had change for a dollar. "But if you don't," he added, bending to pick up one of my red kneesocks that my mother had dropped on the floor, "I was also wondering if you might like to go out sometime. The big top is in town."

"No, I don't think so," my mother said, not looking up.

She was pulling wet clothes from a washing machine and shoving them into one of the empty dryers across the aisle. Gus and I were sitting on the closed lid of another washer, eating jelly beans and watching her. Our own washing machine at home was broken, which was why we were at the Laundromat. We had never been there before. It was eight thirty at night, the Saturday before Easter, and besides the man with no shirt and a lady and her baby, we were the only people there.

"No, you don't have four quarters or no, you don't want to go out with me?" the man asked. He put one hand over his heart. He was still holding my red kneesock and his crumpled dollar bill.

"Either," my mother said, shoving our wet clothes. "Both."

"Well, think about it." The man handed my sock back to my mother. "And if you decide something different, I'll be right over there reading *Time* magazine."

He pointed to one of the metal folding chairs in the corner, next to the pay phone. Above the phone was a list of Laundromat rules. The first rule was that you couldn't wash sleeping bags or bath mats. The second one was no loitering. The fifth one was that you had to be wearing shoes and a shirt at all times.

I watched the man go back to the corner and pick up his magazine. He crossed his legs and began to read. A minute later, his head dipped to one side and he started to snore.

"He's supposed to be wearing a shirt," I whispered to Gus.

"Oh, I know that." Gus took a green jelly bean from the cellophane sack and stared up at the buzzing fluorescent lights. "It's so bright in here," he said, squinting.

By then all of our clothes were spinning around in slow circles. My mother had filled five dryers all in a row, and now she was standing, leaning against one of them, looking out the dark front glass and into the night.

I jumped down off the washing machine and went and stood in front of her. I pressed my shoulder to the warm door of the dryer and stared out the window, too. There was nothing to see except our own reflections. My mother put her fingers in my hair, smoothing it. Gus was drumming his heels on the side of the washing machine and it made the sound of something big and hollow and empty. The lady with the baby had finished folding her towels and stacking them into a laundry basket. She lay the baby in its blanket on top of the stacks and carried it all out the front door like that, with the baby still asleep. For a second, there was a push of cold air after she'd gone.

"What's wrong with that guy?" I asked my mother. I could see the reflection of the snoring man in the window.

"Probably quite a few things," she said. She kept smoothing my hair. "Next week I have to sign some papers," she told me.

I felt her taking a long breath. I didn't turn around. I could see her face perfectly in the dark glass. Gus was still kicking his heels against the dryer.

"I have to sign the divorce papers," she said. "And I've been trying and trying to find the way to tell you."

My back still to her, she put both of her hands on top of my head and shut her eyes. I watched her do this the way I sometimes watched strangers in the grocery store whisper something to themselves or steal a grape or a hard candy from the open bins when they thought no one was looking. It was something too secret to see. I looked down at the square linoleum tiles and back at the window.

"I haven't seen him," my mother went on, talking faster, her eyes open now. "It's all been done through the lawyers. All of it. I know you're wondering that, but no, I haven't seen him. I've just had to go ahead and do this because I'm not going to pretend anymore, and because I don't think anyone should. If he's not coming back, we shouldn't . . ."

I turned and wrapped my arms around my mother's waist, burying my face in her sweater. Gus had jumped down from the washing machine and was yanking at her sleeve. "What's wrong with Annie?" he asked.

"Shhh, there," my mother told him. "See if our clothes are dry yet."

Gus cupped his face to the glass front of one of the dryers. "I can't tell," he said.

"Hey!" the man with no shirt called from across the Laundromat. "Do any of you all happen to know what time it is? I left my watch out on Route 37."

Gus pointed to the glowing clock on the wall.

"Jesus!" the man shouted. "How'd it get to be so late?" He got up and ran over to one of the stopped clothes dryers, throwing it open hard. "My wardrobe has been nearly incinerated!" He grabbed a sweatshirt and some pants, socks, and underwear, pulling all of it close to his chest and carrying it over to the folding table. "I'm going to have to speak to the management!" he called to us, after a minute.

My mother knelt in front of me. "I'm so sorry, so sorry." She leaned her forehead against mine. We weren't crying.

"Please get up," Gus said, stamping one of his boots. "I'm ready to go home."

All our dryers had stopped spinning. My mother rose to her feet. The three of us stood there in a little circle, blinking at one another under all that bright light.

"Okay?" she asked.

The man was dressed by then. He was even wearing a coat and a knitted hat and a scarf. I didn't notice any of this until he was right up next to us, spreading his big arms wide and draping them across our shoulders. That close, he smelled like bleach and like ashes, like something on fire. There were tiny lines at the corners of his mouth and his eyes were a beautiful color of blue.

"Happy Easter," he whispered. "It's been a pleasure getting to know you."

I HAVE SOME FRIENDS

For one thing, Shepherd Nash tried too hard. That made me almost hate him. It started with the gifts—a jigsaw puzzle of a clown that Gus and I put together in about five seconds with our eyes shut, two squirt guns, a glow-in-the-dark map of the galaxy, shiny-covered books about boys and girls and their horses, a box of caramel corn that tasted as if it had been left out in the rain. That one we ripped into right when he was standing there and chewed it hard with our mouths opened wide. We were still full from dinner, but we put on a good show. It felt like eating pencil erasers, and he watched us from the doorway. "Oh!" he said, catching his thumbs in his belt loops and rocking back on his heels. "I'm so glad you like it." That was when I could tell he wouldn't last long.

But he did, for three more dates: inflatable beach balls, waxy crayons, a stuffed monkey. Once I woke up and heard his truck starting late at night. That was number five. On the sixth he brought us another box of caramel corn, even bigger. By then he believed we loved it. We worked our jaws and ate with our heads hung. I had the feeling he wanted us to start thinking of him as some kind of uncle.

As we chewed, my mother got ready in the bathroom. She took her time choosing an outfit or doing things to her hair and eyes. Later, she'd come out blinking like an animal caught in someone's headlights, smelling of peppermint and cut flowers. Her bracelets would flash as he helped her on with her coat, and when she bent to kiss us good-bye, she'd leave smears of color on our cheeks. But first there'd be some waiting, and after giving us our gifts, Shepherd would use those minutes to ask Gus and me about school or our hobbies. After five dates he knew it all—Gus was in kindergarten, I was in third grade; we liked animals and TV shows about police—but nothing stopped him.

"So what have you kids been up to?" Shepherd asked when we were halfway through our act with the latest box of caramel corn. From behind the closed door, my mother's hair dryer sounded like a bee caught in a jar. Shepherd smiled at me. One of his eyebrows twitched.

I swallowed a big, sticky lump of corn and lied easily. "Nothing," I told him. Gus kept chewing, showing off his new missing tooth. It had been in the front and left an open space the shape of a broken window.

"Huh," Shepherd said, jingling his car keys against his leg. He stared at Gus's mouth.

My mother had shut off the hair dryer and you could hear water running, something snapping. "I've been busy," Shepherd told us, settling into a chair and making himself at home. He stretched his feet to where Gus and I were sitting on the Oriental carpet. His boots were covered in fresh mud. It was the end of spring. I knew he wanted us to ask, "Doing what?" but there was no way. I shoveled a fistful of gummy kernels. I knew enough: Shepherd was an electrician but he called himself an artist and lived downtown, up over the ice cream parlor. He sang at people's weddings or if they had a big party. He played the guitar and the piano and wore a suit. That was his art. All the rest of the time Shepherd fixed people's wiring or worked on fuse boxes. My mother met him when he came to install track lights in our living room. Shepherd had moved from Chicago a few months before. No one else in our small town was an artist. There were some other electricians. He didn't fool me.

"Busy, busy," Shepherd told us. "It's gratifying, really."

The three of us eyed one another. I stared at the sharp creases in Shepherd's pants. I could tell that he'd ironed his blue jeans.

"Thanks!" Gus said suddenly, spitting a piece of caramel corn against Shepherd's leg. It stayed there for a second, the size of a dime. As Shepherd brushed it away the phone started ringing.

"Listen," he whispered. "Oh dear." He got up, shaking his ankle, and walked down the hall to the bathroom door. "Knock, knock." He bent down to talk near the keyhole. "Telephone!"

"Help Mr. Nash!" my mother shouted to us through the door. That was what we were supposed to call him. In the kitchen, the phone rang and rang.

"Telephone!" Shepherd said again, pressing his lips to the doorknob.

"Yoo-hoo, Annie!" my mother yelled to me.

Gus and I chewed. We wanted to see Shepherd answer the phone.

"All right!" My mother threw open the bathroom door and clattered toward the kitchen. She was wearing a dress like the ones women in India have on in *National Geographic* and her hair was up in a bun. Lately, she had been talking about getting a job, and she was experimenting with new ways to dress. Most of her outfits didn't look like things other grown-ups wore to work. She kept her back to us all, and Shepherd tiptoed to where Gus and I were sitting.

"Gee," he whispered. "I never know what to do in these sorts of situations."

"Okay." Gus nodded, even though I knew he didn't understand what Shepherd had said. Then we were quiet, listening to my mother talk.

"That's too bad," she was saying. "You should stay in bed. Certainly not. Yes, I'm sorry, too."

Shepherd wrinkled his forehead.

"That was Grace," my mother told us after a minute, coming into the room. "She claims to be sick, but I can't help thinking she's not telling the truth. I'm a little surprised. Anyway, she can't make it."

Grace Nanagost was our babysitter. She wore big silver earrings and had a scar above her lip. Sometimes, when she was watching TV with Gus and me, she'd take sips out of a paper bag she kept in her jacket pocket and say things like, "If I had babies, they sure wouldn't look like you." I never told my mother about this because she had already fired Grace once for being drunk on the job.

"She can't come *at all?*" Shepherd caught my mother's

elbow and looked serious. Gus and I kept eating. My tongue was stuck to the inside of my mouth.

"No," my mother said.

Gus grinned like a jack-o'-lantern. He was afraid of Grace.

"Well!" Shepherd smiled and stared at the wall above our heads. It was hard to say if he was really excited or trying to be. "Here we are!"

"This is it. The end," I whispered to Gus while Shepherd and my mother discussed canceling their dinner reservations. "You watch."

"The end," Gus said, sighing a long, caramel-smelling breath.

"Chew," I whispered.

W hat happened was that Shepherd decided to take us all on the date and, since it was the last, I kept quiet. We rode in his truck, which had his name in big letters on its side: SHEPHERD NASH—VOCAL ARTIST/ELECTRICAL ENGINEER. There was also a phone number and a lightning bolt. My mother acted like she was riding in a regular car and even hummed along with the tape recorder set up on the dashboard in place of a radio. Luckily, I didn't have to wait long for Shepherd to do something. As he drove us to the movie theater, he told us the whole plot. I elbowed Gus to make sure he noticed. "It's a huge shark," Shepherd said, turning onto Hill Street. "Giant. I mean, absolutely the biggest. 'Grand,' they call it. No, 'Great.' And it keeps on biting people in half. Swimmers mostly. Then a young scientist . . ."

"Biting?" my mother asked. She and Shepherd were holding

hands in the front, and Gus and I were on the bench seat beside them, buckled in tight. The back of the truck was filled with piles of metal parts and screwdrivers, a sign from a rest area, a guitar, a rolling microphone and its stand. Everything clanked around curves. Shepherd was a terrible driver.

"Uh-huh." Shepherd continued: "So this young scientist takes an interest in . . ."

"Biting?" my mother said again, removing her hand from Shepherd's. My mother sounded surprised. "I thought perhaps the victims were pulled under."

"Nope." Shepherd pumped the brakes when we came to the stoplight by the grocery store. "I've seen this, you know. I'm only warning you."

My mother leaned over and said something into Shepherd's ear. "Um, I don't think so," Shepherd told her. "None that I remember, anyway."

During the movie I kept my face covered whenever someone started screaming. Gus sat on his heels and screamed along with the people being bitten. In one part, he even got down on the floor with the old gum and empty drink cups. When we came outside, Shepherd wanted to make up for it.

"A buddy of mine's band is playing down at the Cedar Inn," he said to my mother, holding open the truck door. In the moonlight, you could see that the lightning bolt on the side was painted with a special sparkling silver. "How about if we go and listen to some music? It might calm them." He gave Gus and me a hopeful look, like when someone asks to borrow a quarter.

"It's past their bedtime now," my mother said when we were all loaded.

"Aw, they can sleep in," Shepherd begged. "Just this once? It'll be great!"

"Children don't sleep in," my mother told him, rearranging her hair in the rearview mirror.

Gus and I yawned as Shepherd clasped my mother's hand to his chest.

"Please?" he said. "It would mean the world to me."

"All right," she sighed. "I suppose."

I didn't say a word. I could tell it was the end, and we went to a place where Shepherd knew the owner. We got a table up front, away from all the men holding beer bottles and playing pool. Shepherd found a couple of old phone books for Gus to sit on. I sat on menus and a wadded-up coat. We ordered Shirley Temples with extra cherries, and when the music started Shepherd asked my mother to dance. He held her waist and they shuffled in a circle near our chairs. Every time they did a turn, Shepherd winked at us. My mother looked like she was asleep. The dark room was packed, but Gus and I were the only children there. The big clock on the wall read nine forty-five. "I hate Grace," Gus said when Shepherd and my mother were dancing their second dance.

"Why?" I asked him, eating a cherry.

"Because she looks so mean," Gus said.

I turned the way Gus was and saw Grace wiggling her hips

and snapping her fingers over her head near the far wall. She was wearing a tight white dress. When she caught sight of us staring at her, she quit snapping and took a long drink from the glass she was holding. She gave us a wave. By then, Shepherd and my mother were back at the table.

"Grace says hi," Gus told them.

"Fine," my mother said. "It's time for you two to be home in bed." She wiped above her lip with the tiny square napkin from under Shepherd's beer.

I turned and waved at Grace. I was happy to see her.

"That *is* your babysitter," Shepherd told my mother.

We all looked. Grace was back to snapping. "Ha!" my mother said. "Never again."

We took the long way out, the four of us forming a human chain, so that my mother could have a word with Grace. When we got over to her, Grace put one elbow on the jukebox and saluted.

"Look here," my mother said, pointing at Grace's puffy chest. "You aren't sick one bit."

"It was a twenty-four-hour bug!" Grace shouted above the music. She had her hair in two long braids and her forehead was shiny. "What do you expect?"

"I had dinner reservations." My mother put her face near Grace's. "I've fired you once already."

Grace rolled her shoulders and shimmied in place.

"Hey, Shep," Grace said, turning to Shepherd like he was an old best friend. "Some woman was looking for you earlier." She took a sip from her sweaty glass and made her eyes round.

"Oh?" Shepherd said.

"Yep," Grace told him, while we all stood holding hands and the band played loud. "Redhead. Kind of nutty."

Shepherd glanced at my mother. "She must have been looking for someone else."

"Is your name Shepherd?" Grace snorted. "Are you an e-lec-tri-ci-an?"

"Hmm," Shepherd said, stuffing his hands in his pockets.

"Do you still want me next Friday?" Grace asked my mother. "I expect I'll feel better by then."

My mother didn't answer but pushed Gus and me toward the door. "Bye, Annie! Bye, Gus!" Grace yelled.

Shepherd kept his head low and followed us past the pool tables.

"Nutty?" my mother asked, when we were under the stars. She said it loud as if she was still trying to talk over the music. Gus and I hung back, the last two links in our human chain, while she and Shepherd whispered next to the truck.

"That was fun," Gus said, whistling through his missing tooth. "I like dates."

"It was terrible," I said, trying to be happy. I could tell that things were turning out even worse than I thought they might and I wasn't sure why.

"No, no, no," Shepherd was whispering. "She lives in Chicago. I would have told you." Shepherd made his voice even lower. "It almost wasn't legal."

"I'm in shock," my mother hissed. "And I hear about it from a babysitter?"

"I should have mentioned it," Shepherd said. "I can see that now."

On the drive home, no one spoke. We listened to the electrical equipment slide against the guitar in the back of the truck. Shepherd tried once. "Hey," he said, when we were by the post office. "Does anyone want ice cream?" Gus and I were still stuffed from all the caramel corn, the jujubes at the shark movie, the seven maraschino cherries. We stayed quiet.

"Ice cream?" Shepherd offered.

"Please," my mother said, and I knew that was the last of him.

He showed up the next morning with a big bouquet of purple flowers tied with a bow. We could see him coming from where we were eating breakfast at the dining room table. Since it was Saturday, my mother had made us waffles, and when the doorbell rang we were just cutting into them. Gus tipped the syrup bottle that was shaped like an old woman and held it high while Shepherd sulked on the front porch.

"I'm ignoring him," my mother informed us. Her eyes were pink.

"I like that guy," Gus said, chewing.

Shepherd was peeking in the window, his hand cupped to the glass. He waved the bouquet.

"Not me," I said.

"Okay, eat your waffles," my mother told us, taking a sip of coffee. She moved her chair so that her back was to Shepherd. "Is he gone?" she asked after a second.

"No," I told her. Shepherd was frowning and had stopped shaking the flowers but he was still there.

"Dammit," my mother said, rubbing her temples.

Shepherd began to knock.

"What lady was looking for him?" I asked my mother.

"Some friend." My mother turned and glared at the tapping noise. "Knock all you want!" she told Shepherd.

"A friend?" I asked. I thought of my friends, Beth and Katie, and how we all wanted horses and to get our ears pierced.

"Yes," my mother said, and the knocking stopped. Then: "I'm not speaking to you!"

"I have some friends," Gus said, even though he only had one friend, Tommy Drake, and even that was not for certain.

"Yes, you do." My mother patted his head. "And it's important," she told us, "to *be* a good friend as well as to have them."

You couldn't help notice Shepherd. Both his hands were pressed to the window and he looked like he might cry.

"Oh please," my mother said, when we pointed this out. "He's a grown man. A grown man!" she added, facing Shepherd. She drank her coffee. "I won't even get into the rest of it," she assured us. "He knows it's finished."

Shepherd stayed on the porch all morning. My mother did laundry, and Gus and I watched cartoons and then *Perry Mason*. During commercials, we checked on what Shepherd was doing next. "Sleeping," Gus would say, peering out, or, "Scratching his hair." When I looked, he had his face in his arms, bent over the railing. Another time he was reading a book, the flowers wilting near his feet.

We lived on a road without many people—Lake Michigan on one side, trees on the other. Our closest neighbors, the Slocums, lived behind a tall cedar hedge. Probably no one else heard when he started to sing. My mother was vacuuming upstairs. "He sounds like the radio," Gus said. We turned down the TV and listened. It was true; Shepherd had a perfect voice—better than any record. Gus and I crouched under the window to hear. He sang three songs—all of them about hearts or people being sad. He knew every word and they came out high and clear. Before he started each song, he'd give an introduction: "This is to that special woman!" he'd yell. "I dedicate this to the love of my life!"

After the third song, I had forgiven Shepherd for everything. My mother wasn't as impressed. She couldn't concentrate enough to vacuum. "Come on. We're going to the bank," she told us, grabbing her purse. "And then to the grocery store. I can't think with that noise."

Outside, it was a bright, sunny day. When Shepherd saw us, he started song number four but quit after only one line. We followed my mother, stepping over the bouquet. By then, I was feeling terrible. I knew that I had cursed Shepherd and all his trying. Whatever happened was probably my fault.

"Give me another chance!" Shepherd pleaded as we made our way down the front walk.

I'd never seen a grown man get down on his knees and make fists at the sky, but this was what Shepherd did, right in the driveway. It went on for a minute or so.

"You're married," my mother told him.

Gus and I stared at Shepherd as he clenched and un-clenched his pink fingers and crushed the toes of his boots against the hard cement. He didn't look married.

"Do you deny it?" my mother asked.

"Well," Shepherd said. He stood and brushed off his jeans. "Can I buy you lunch?"

"We went on five dates!" my mother screamed at him.

"Six," I whispered.

"I hear your wife is looking for you." My mother sniffed and tried to swat Shepherd with her purse but he jumped.

As we backed the car up and maneuvered it around Shep-herd's electrical truck, my mother set him straight. "You've ter-rified the children," she told him, rolling down her window. "And you won't be here when we get back."

"I'm not terrified," I said. "Really."

In the backseat, Gus nodded his head.

"You could be." My mother put on her sunglasses. "He ought to behave."

"She's a friend!" Shepherd shouted, but he got out of our path. Gus and I waved good-bye.

"Ha!" my mother said to us when we were safely down the road. "Some kind of friend."

"What kind?" I asked.

We turned down Lake View Road. I could tell we were only driving to drive.

"Mr. Nash is married to this friend of his," my mother snapped.

"*I* wouldn't marry my friend," I told her, feeling sorry for him. "I'd marry someone else."

"Of course you would," my mother said, lighting a cigarette she had dug out from the bottom of her bag. "That's my
point. It's a *big* mistake to marry a friend."

"You don't smoke," I told my mother, but she ignored me.

For a mile the three of us were quiet. I stared out at the light
green hills, the broken fences and black-and-white cows.

My mother went on: "They got married when he lived in
Chicago. They are still married. And now she's come up here
for a visit—out of the blue—to try to work things out. It seems
he forgot to tell me."

"Oh," Gus said. "I'm glad about that."

"No, you're not," I reminded him.

Shepherd called and called, but my mother refused to even
speak to him. She hung up the phone the minute she heard
his voice. The strange thing was, I felt saddest knowing there
would be no more awful gifts. No plastic squirt guns to leak
all over the rug, no crayons to leave an oily film all over the
table, no stale caramel corn to chew while he watched. For a
week, Gus and I went to school and came home knowing that
on Friday there would be nothing new. And it was more than
gifts; it was Shepherd himself. Now that he was gone, I only
wanted him to come back. For some reason, it had worked
that way.

On Thursday afternoon, we got out the inflatable beach
balls Shepherd had given us and played catch in the yard. After a
few minutes we ended up using them like chairs. While my
mother paced in the house, Gus and I tried sitting on the beach

balls, balancing above the wet lawn, wondering about Shepherd. "It's my fault," I admitted. "I never wanted him here."

"I miss him quite a bit," Gus said.

"Me, too." I squashed my beach ball and kept thinking. Everywhere blossoms were blooming, throwing their curled petals down like bits of torn paper, and the grass glowed dark green. We watched a robin yanking a worm.

"What do you think he's doing right now?" Gus asked.

"Singing," I lied. "Dancing."

"Good," Gus said.

"I feel terrible." I stared at the house, trying to catch a glimpse of my mother in the window. Gus slid off his beach ball. He walked around the yard on his knees, waving his small fists at the clouds. "Give me another chance!" he yelled.

"Don't bother," I said. "You don't look like him at all."

After that, we lay on our backs staring at the sky.

"He'll show up," I said, trying to believe it.

"Maybe if that lady'd quit following us, he would," Gus said.

"What lady?" I rolled onto my stomach.

"The lady who follows us everywhere." Gus poked his tongue through the space in the front of his mouth. "To school, the grocery store. When we got pizza."

"What?" I asked. I hadn't seen any lady. All of a sudden my stomach hurt, worse than when I'd eaten the caramel corn.

"The lady," Gus said, pointing down the street toward a clump of overgrown lilac bushes wedged between rows of maple trees. When I squinted, I could see part of the front bumper of a car sticking out from behind the drooping branches.

Gus and I left our beach balls and began tiptoeing down the

road. As we got closer, I saw that the car was round and orange; a VW bug. The person inside was crouched in back of the steering wheel. You could only see a tangle of red hair. When Gus said, "Hey, lady!" the car started right up and took off fast. In a second it had vanished completely. All that was left was a big circle of bent weeds and a paper cup with bubble-gum-colored kisses around the rim.

"That lady," Gus said.

When we got back in the house, my mother was yelling into the phone. "I told you I don't want you tomorrow or ever!" she was saying. "You've ruined a perfectly good relationship!" She was smoking again and wrapping the phone cord tight around her wrist. "Look, Grace," she said, "you knew exactly what you were doing." She stubbed out her cigarette in the potted palm by the couch and held up one finger. "Of course I would have found out sooner or later. But not from you!" She covered the mouthpiece with her hand. "What, kids?" she asked. The color around her eyes had smeared and there was a streak of dried mustard down the front of her shirt. She lit another cigarette. "What?" she whispered.

"There's a car and it's orange and . . . ," Gus began, still panting from our run to the house.

"Nothing," I told her, yanking his arm.

"I'm talking to Mom!" Gus said, pulling free. He stamped his tennis shoes and waved the paper cup with the lipstick marks. The knees of his jeans were bright green from his crawling on the lawn. I wanted to pinch him hard.

"What's the problem?" my mother asked. She held the phone out away from her ear.

"Oh, that lady who's been following us," Gus told her. He jumped on one foot, enjoying his story. "She was in her orange car out by the lilac trees, but Annie scared her away."

"I did not!" I yelled. I grabbed Gus's shoulder, but he dodged me and hid behind a chair.

"Grace, I have to go," my mother said, and then hung the phone up on the couch cushions.

"Okay, what," she said, taking a puff.

"A lady is following us," I told her. "And she has red hair and probably pierced ears."

"Following?" my mother asked. She sounded tired.

"Yeah," Gus said from behind the chair. His hand appeared and tried to roll the paper cup across the Oriental rug. The cup stopped in the middle, pale and alone.

"Following?" my mother asked again, staring at the cup. "What do you mean?"

"She followed us to school. Then when we went to the store. Then—" Gus said.

"Why didn't you say something?" my mother asked, jumping up. She went to the window. "This could be dangerous."

Gus crept from behind the chair and shrugged. My mother bent and picked up the paper cup. "This is unbelievable," she said, examining the lip marks. "I have no idea what that woman wants with me. Following us! Some nerve!"

"What did she look like?" my mother asked, pacing around the room.

Gus gave a long, detailed description that was all lies. "Tall," he added, finishing up. "And curly."

"Wrong," I said, but they ignored me.

"Ha!" my mother laughed. "This is classic!" She lit another cigarette. One was still burning on the edge of the coffee table.

"Yes," Gus agreed, pretending to know.

"Well, I've heard enough," my mother told us, lighting a third cigarette while she held the second in her left hand. She took turns puffing on both. "And I won't put up with this sort of monkey business, you can bet!"

By then, the orange car was back, cruising slowly past the front porch. My mother kept smoking, not noticing. "Mr. Nash and his friend should *both* behave!" she said. "Let this be a lesson in bad behavior!"

The car did a turn and came to a stop by the mouth of our driveway. "Furthermore," my mother continued, her back to the window, "he's an electrician! I was never in love with him. Period." She sat down on the sofa. "Well, maybe a little. To be honest, the whole thing's a mess. What do you kids want for dinner?"

"Fried clams," Gus said, waving at the car. I stood next to him and looked out.

"You need vegetables," my mother corrected. She pressed out one of her cigarettes and put her free hand over her eyes.

A second later, Shepherd's truck pulled alongside the orange VW. He began yelling down at the driver. They argued back and forth, revving their engines. We couldn't really hear what they were saying. Shepherd leaned way out of his window and jabbed his finger in the air.

"There he is," Gus whispered. "Back again."

"I suppose clams are healthy enough," my mother said finally, smoking the last of the second cigarette while the third smoldered on the table. Her head was settled on the sofa cushions and her eyes were shut.

When I turned back to the window, Shepherd's friend had gotten out of her car and was smacking her hand on the hood of his truck. It sounded like the beavers Gus and I had seen on a nature show the week before who whacked their tails on water to communicate with each other. Shepherd locked his door and stayed in the truck while his friend slapped and swatted down one whole side.

"That reminds me—" I began to say.

"Yeah, I know," Gus said.

"She's not so tall," I told him after a minute. "You were wrong about that."

Gus shrugged. "What is that noise?" my mother asked, her eyes still closed. "Can someone bring me two aspirin and a glass of water?"

There was no way Gus was budging from watching the lady hitting Shepherd's truck, so I went to get the aspirin. By the time I'd gone to the medicine cabinet and gotten a glass of water, Shepherd and his friend were gone. "Thanks," my mother said, swallowing the pills.

"What happened?" I asked Gus, but he only grinned.

"From now on," my mother told us, sitting up, "I want you to tell me when you see that woman again."

Gus nodded.

"Keep me informed," my mother said, walking toward the kitchen, "about anything that looks unusual. Anytime you see something that doesn't look quite right, let me know."

"Okay," Gus told her. "Let me know."

"Hey," I said, but no one seemed to care. Gus had turned on the TV, and my mother was banging in the refrigerator. "Hey," I said again, softly. "I saw something not quite right." I took the last cigarette from the coffee table and dropped it into the plant. It sent up a thin thread of smoke and I watched it until I was certain that it was really out.

"I don't see any clams in here!" my mother called from the kitchen.

I knew that I was on my own when it came to getting Shepherd back.

Nothing happened all that night, even though I lay awake a long time, listening for cars. The phone never even rang. On the way to school the next morning, my mother kept look-ing in the rearview mirror but no one was following us. "You might have been imagining this," she suggested as she turned into the school parking lot. She was wearing her nightgown under her raincoat and she looked annoyed.

"No!" Gus shouted, rattling his Hardy Boys lunch box. I didn't bother to add any more.

"Well, you think about it. There are a lot of orange cars," my mother said. "I'll pick you up here at three fifteen."

I couldn't concentrate, not even on recess. Nothing seemed interesting or even halfway unusual. I gave up at noon and began to wait for the last bell. While we were supposed to be reading in *Our Big Blue World* books, I tried to make lists on wide-lined paper of places Shepherd's friend might be hiding out. I couldn't think of any. When we were finally allowed to leave, I went and stood on the sidewalk in front of the big doors. Gus was already there with a pack of other younger kids. He was bragging about the orange car. "It tried to run over me," he was saying.

"You're such a liar," I told him, which only made him talk more.

As he was starting the second part of his story, Shepherd's truck pulled up in the Fire/No Parking lane. The silver lightning bolt glistened in the sun like the underside of a trout. You could hear Tommy Drake catch his breath. "That guy sang at my parents' Christmas party," Tommy told us. "He was terrible."

"He has a perfect voice," I said, but everyone was staring at the truck.

Shepherd leaned over and opened the passenger-side door. "Hello, children," he said. "May I give you a ride home?"

I hopped right up, but Gus stayed put. "Mom's coming to get us," he pouted, staring at his shoes.

"Tommy can tell her that Shepherd gave us a ride," I said.

Gus shook his head like the coward I knew he was. "Come on, Gus," Shepherd said. "I'd just like to talk to you two for a minute. I want to explain a few things."

Gus didn't move. "Aw, come on," Shepherd said again. "If you're not careful, I might start singing." This made Gus jump, and I helped him buckle in.

We sat on the seat next to Shepherd. He pretended to be our taxi driver. "Where to?" he joked. Gus and I were quiet. "Seriously," Shepherd began, when we were out of the school lot, "I really need to talk. I need to be heard! I have some things I'd like to say."

"Okay," I said, preparing myself. "You can."

"Well, for starters," Shepherd told us, "I care a lot about what you think of me. A lot! You kids are like family to me. And I'd hate for you to think I'd wronged you in any way."

Gus elbowed me as we drove past the grocery store. *"Wronged?"* he whispered.

"Shhh," I said.

"My own family! And I don't have to tell you that your mother is the woman of my dreams. Now she won't even speak to me!" Shepherd leaned forward over the steering wheel and tilted his chin to the sky. "My dream woman! Life was perfect!"

"Well," Gus said.

"Shut up or else," I told him.

"Then this whole mess with old Sally," Shepherd continued. "Who'd think she'd show up out of nowhere?"

"Sally?" I asked.

"My wife, Sally," Shepherd said. "Hey, I can see that this might take awhile. How about if I get you kids some ice cream and then we can really talk?"

"Good," Gus agreed. "I'd like some ice cream."

"I don't know." I pulled at my windbreaker zipper and thought about what Shepherd had said. "You're sure you're married?" I asked him.

"Yes, technically." He parked the truck in front of the ice cream parlor. "More or less."

"My parents were married," Gus told Shepherd.

"Oh, I know," Shepherd said, his voice softer now. "I know."

We followed Shepherd inside. The woman behind the counter knew Shepherd because he lived upstairs. "Any flavor," she told Gus and me. "On the house." She winked at Shepherd.

Gus ordered blue moon, a triple dip. I had pistachio. "That looks great!" Shepherd said, trying to make his voice sound excited. He wiped off one of the little round tables in the front with his shirtsleeve and we sat down, stashing our lunch boxes near our feet.

"We saw you yesterday," Gus said between mouthfuls.

"Oh?" Shepherd looked out at the street.

"You were yelling at the orange car."

Shepherd sighed and put his face flat on the table. "I'm sorry you had to witness that. Was your mother looking, by any chance?"

"No," I told him.

"She was smoking," Gus added.

Shepherd sat up and slapped his hand over his heart. A screwdriver was sticking out of his breast pocket but he shoved it out of the way. "Maybe there's still hope," he said.

"Maybe," Gus said, licking his blue cone.

I was getting impatient. "So what about your wife?" I asked Shepherd. "She was hiding by our house."

"I won't lie," Shepherd said. "Sally's the curious sort." He scratched his chin and coughed. "Listen, I need your help. I'm a desperate man! You've got to help me. How can I get your mother to take me back?"

Gus and I stopped eating our ice cream and stared at Shepherd. There were dark rings under his eyes and he was growing a beard. You could see that he probably hadn't slept for a while.

"You're married," I told him.

"You look tired," Gus said, patting Shepherd's sleeve.

"Lord!" Shepherd cried, shaking his fists at the ceiling.

The woman behind the counter flashed us a dirty look. "None of that talk in here," she warned.

Shepherd put his head back down on the table while Gus and I finished our cones.

"I am married, it's true," Shepherd admitted from his resting position. "But Sally was a friend. We only lived together for a couple of months. We were basically *children* when we got hitched."

Gus swallowed hard when Shepherd said the word *children*. "How could that happen?" he whispered.

"The ceremony was performed by a guy who got his reverendhood out of the back of a magazine! In Mexico! I'd have to say that I was quite drunk. Does that sound legal to you?"

"Yes," Gus said.

"Be quiet," I told him.

Shepherd blew his nose on a napkin from the metal dispenser near his forehead. "Well, you're right, it is legal. Some surprise! Sally got a lawyer to look into it. She's out at that motel on M-119 right now, thinking of ways to take me to the cleaners." He sat up. "It's an expression," he told us. "She wants all my money. Which is precisely zero dollars, to be exact."

"You probably love her," I told Shepherd.

"Maybe a long time ago. Maybe for about ten minutes," Shepherd said, blowing his nose again. "But my point is that she was always just a good friend, nothing more."

Since Gus and I were done with our cones there was nothing to do except sit with our hands clasped in front of us, listening to Shepherd sniffling and groaning. The clock on the wall read four twenty-five. "Have you ever heard of such a mess?" Shepherd asked finally.

Gus opened wide, showing his blue tongue. "My front tooth fell out," he told Shepherd.

"What would you do?" Shepherd pleaded, ignoring Gus's mouth. "I'm asking you, what would you do?"

While the three of us were thinking about this, my mother pulled up outside next to Shepherd's truck. She didn't even bother to park but left the car running right in the middle of the street. When she got inside the ice cream parlor, you could see that her eyes were red and puffy, as if she'd been crying. We all sat still, waiting to see what she'd do. She let out a big breath and dropped her purse on the floor. She worked her jaw up and down. "Thief," she said.

"Hey, now!" the counterwoman yelled, leaning over the ice cream case. She adjusted her glasses and scowled at my mother. "I already warned you all once."

Shepherd tried to stand.

"Wait outside," my mother told Gus and me.

We gathered our lunch boxes and jackets. "Thanks for the ice cream," Gus said to Shepherd. He said it like he really meant it. I wanted to say something, too, but I couldn't think of what. As we walked to the door, I kept turning around to see what they were doing. My mother had picked up her purse and was using napkins to wipe her eyes.

When we were out on the sidewalk Gus let loose. "Why are *you* crying?" I asked.

He mumbled and hugged his lunch box over his chest. We huddled near a parked van while Shepherd and my mother silently moved their mouths on the other side of the glass. It had started to sprinkle so we put up our hoods. Little drops of water blew against our faces. "He could be like a father to us," Gus said finally.

Standing there in the rainy May afternoon, I suddenly knew it was the thing I'd been thinking all along. I also knew that it would somehow never quite happen.

"Maybe," I said.

After a minute, Gus quit crying and we leaned against a telephone pole. A few people honked at our car, which was now stalled in the middle of the street, but then they went around. Shepherd and my mother sat. They faced each other across the tiny table.

"She would have found out sooner or later," I said.

"It'll be okay," Gus decided. "He can buy her a snack."

We put our lunch boxes down and stood on them to get a different view. My mother was talking a lot and waving her arms. Shepherd was agreeing.

"This is good," I said, pointing out the way Shepherd was inching his chair closer to my mother's. "He's trying."

I didn't even hear Shepherd's friend walking up beside us. When I turned, she was standing close to me, staring at Shepherd and my mother, too. "We've almost met" was how she put it, not quite turning to look at us.

She had her red hair in a ponytail, and she gave us her freckly hand to shake hello, but I wouldn't. I thought she'd been watching us the whole time we'd been eating ice cream with Shepherd. "I don't care," I said suddenly. "I don't care." Since we were standing on our lunch boxes, I came to her shoulder.

"I wanted to meet you," Sally stammered. "To see what you were like. All of you." She looked us up and down. "So." She tried to laugh but it came out like a cough. "Here we are."

"You're the one with the orange car," Gus said.

Sally nodded.

The three of us watched Shepherd and my mother silently talking. "I had to take vacation time to do this. I work for a veterinarian," Sally confided, settling against the telephone pole. Her hair was already soaked with rain. "I had to leave work, drive up here. I've had some bad luck lately, I can tell you that." She smiled and then started to cry. "Shepherd was always a good guy so I decided to give it another try, see if we could work it out. Think how stupid I feel! He'd practically forgotten we were even married."

For the first time, I stared at Sally. She wasn't beautiful, exactly. She had her arms crossed and her face was turned up toward the rain. A piece of paper that was nailed to the telephone pole caught the wind and fluttered, trapped, above her head. Sally closed her eyes.

"What was I thinking?" she asked us.

"I don't know," I told her.

By then Shepherd had moved his chair all the way around

so that he was right next to my mother. They looked like they were sitting together on a bus or a train, like they were people going somewhere. I tried to forget that I'd ever hated him.

Sally opened her eyes and shook her head. "I'll probably give up now," she said. "That's what I'll probably do."

"It's okay," I told her, stepping off my lunch box. I knew it wasn't true, that it wasn't okay. Gus hopped down off his lunch box, too, and touched Sally's speckled hand. We stood there, the three of us reflected in the window of the ice cream parlor, our ghost bodies overlapping those of Shepherd and my mother in one big blur. It was the end, but we waited together, for the next thing.

PORCUPINES

My mother hired Susie Medicinehat to clean house, but she ended up doing a lot more than just some dusting. I could tell that Susie had the job even before she opened her mouth and said anything about porcupines. From the first time the rusted-out blue pickup truck dropped her off in our driveway and she hammered on the front door with a hard fist, I felt that she somehow belonged in our house. It wasn't like there were a lot of people lined up waiting for the job. In fact, Susie was our first and only hope. But my mother went ahead and asked her some job interview–like questions about her past experiences in the housecleaning business, and if she minded taking care of my brother, Gus, and me once in a while.

Susie cleared her throat and bowed her head like she was studying something really interesting in her lap. Her black hair glistened like the wing of a grackle under the fluorescent kitchen light. "All I ask, Mrs. Child," she said in a gravelly voice, "is that you leave me enough time on the side for my porcupine business."

"Oh, of course!" my mother said, her hand fluttering to her chest. "And please just call me Paige."

"Okay, Paige," Susie said. "Then it's a done deal."

I could tell my mother thought Susie was going to announce something scary, like that she had to have a lot more money or that she could only work once every other week. My mother couldn't take a blow like that in her current state. She was going through a bad time, taking pills that made her seem not all there and driving really fast—living quick and cheap, as my aunt Claire would say—which was the main reason she started looking for a cleaning lady in the first place. I thought she wanted someone to come in and clean up her life.

"Wonderful!" my mother said. She reached out and patted Susie on the arm like they were the best of friends. "Now tell me about your porcupine business."

I saw the wheels turning in my mother's head. My mother had used up most of the money my grandmother left and she had been talking about getting a job. Not any job but the right kind of job. I knew the porcupines sounded right to her.

"I clean and sell the quills in bulk," Susie said, looking up a little.

She had one of those faces that wasn't young or old, pretty or otherwise. She looked tough, but there was something about the way she kept glancing down that made me think she had a lot of secrets.

"Oh," my mother said, like she understood everything. "Where do you get the porcupines?"

"Roadkill mostly," Susie said. "Sometimes my husband, Joe, will hunt one up, but mostly I get them on the road."

"How wonderful!" my mother said. "A sort of 'found art'! And you make a profit, too! Now, let's see. What do you have to do to the porcupines, exactly?"

I was glad to see my mother get excited about something. She hadn't been interested in much for a long time.

"Well," Susie said, crossing her arms and giving my mother a hard look. I could tell she thought my mother was being a little too curious. "You boil them for a few hours and then pull out their quills. That's the long and the short of it."

"So simple," my mother said. "Now what are the quills used for?"

"Quill boxes. Decorations. Tourist stuff." Susie looked back down at her lap.

"This is great," my mother said. "You'll just have to start bringing your porcupines here and showing me the ropes. I could make earrings, baskets, bracelets . . ."

"I don't know," Susie said. "I thought you hired me to clean."

"There'll be time," my mother said, patting Susie on the arm. "We'll make time. You know, I see dead porcupines now and again but I've never thought of *using* them for anything."

"They're not used," Susie said in her gravelly voice. "Their spirits have left their bodies a long time before I ever touch a quill."

"Oh, of course," my mother said, clearing her throat. "I knew *that*."

That afternoon I rode my bike to my aunt Claire's house. I wanted to tell her all about Susie Medicinehat and how she was going to clean our house and give my mother gainful employment at the same time. Aunt Claire, my mother's older sister, worried about my mother all the time. She worried about the way my mother spent her money, about Shepherd Nash, the man my mother had dated, and most of all she worried that my mother was a true black sheep and that she was setting an irreversible bad example for Gus and me. I hadn't told Aunt Claire about the pills and the driving fast, but she probably somehow knew that, too. She knew everything.

When I pulled up in front of her house, she was outside watering her geraniums. She gave me a smile, but I could see she had something to say.

"Annie," she began, brushing her hair back a bit with one of her green-gloved fingers, "I hear Susie Medicinehat has started working for your mother."

"Yes," I said, dangling my toes and balancing on the bike's banana seat. "Who told you?"

"Susie worked for Flopsy Minturn," Aunt Claire said. She jerked on the hose and started to water the English ivy.

"Oh," I said.

Flopsy Minturn was Aunt Claire's best friend, but I couldn't stand her. She never did anything except play tennis, be president of the garden club, and talk about people through her clenched jaw.

"Flopsy had to let her go," Aunt Claire said, adjusting the hose to the spray setting and moving over to the myrtle.

"Why?" I asked. I hoped that Susie had done something big.

Aunt Claire gave me a hard look. "She was a bad influence on Flopsy's children," she said.

I went to school with the Minturn kids. They were complete sissies. I could tell that Aunt Claire wasn't about to tell me anything else.

"Well, I think Susie is mysterious," I said, trying to balance without letting my toes touch the ground.

"She has about as much mystery as a glass of water," Aunt Claire snapped. "Let's not have any nonsense."

She walked over to the spigot on the side of the house and turned off the hose.

"Now, tell me the truth, Annie," Aunt Claire said, pulling off her gardening gloves. "Is your mother taking better care of herself? I do keep trying to call and get her to do things, but she always says that she's too busy."

"She's great," I lied. "She's just fine."

I decided that it wasn't a good time to bring up the porcupines.

"Well, I hope you're telling me the truth," Aunt Claire said, surveying her garden. "I certainly hope you are."

The next time Susie came to our house, Gus and I were getting ready for school. It was just starting to get light out when I saw the blue pickup truck pull up through the mist in the pine trees surrounding the driveway. I could see that a man was driving the truck but I didn't get a very good look at his face. He wore a baseball hat pulled down to his eyes, and he kept looking off toward the road. Susie got out carrying a transistor radio and a big burlap sack. I opened the front door for her and she headed straight for the hall closet like she'd been there a million times before, hefting the burlap sack as gently as a sleeping baby. Quills poked menacingly through the fabric, shooting off in every direction like crazy arrows, but Susie didn't seem to mind.

"Hold this for a second, would ya." She handed me the sack.

Susie took her time hanging her jacket in the closet. It was red sateen and had THE SPOT BAR written across the back. I knew it was the place with all the motorcycles parked in front, the place where a guy had gotten his ear bitten off in a game of pool last summer. I kept wishing she would hurry up because the bag was heavy. I held it as far away from my body as my arms would reach.

"Don't you worry," Susie said. "It can't bite now."

She laughed to herself a little and then grabbed the sack and moved toward the kitchen.

"Mother up yet?" Susie asked, setting the sack on the counter. She banged around in the kitchen cabinets, looking for something.

"No," I said. I wanted to tell her that my mother had taken half a bottle of aspirin the night before and then said her ears rang and she could see bright flashing colors everywhere she looked, and that this morning she would wake up late, as she had for the last month, and throw her mink coat on over her nightgown and drive Gus and me to school at a dangerous speed.

"She'll be up in a minute," I said. I wanted to tell Susie about my mother's experiments with life, but I didn't know how.

"Pity." Susie frowned. "I wanted her to see this."

She found the giant turkey roaster, the one we used once at Thanksgiving and then never again, and began to fill it with water. She turned the faucet on full force so water sprayed out everywhere.

"I wanted her to see how you have to trim the quills to loosen them up!" she shouted over the water.

She set the pan on the stove and got a pair of rubber gloves from under the sink. She gently slid the porcupine from the sack. It lay on the counter as if it was taking a nap. Susie pushed it over onto its stomach and went to work. "See," she said, taking my mother's best pair of Swiss kitchen scissors. "You have to cut off just the very tips of the quills. That breaks the suction. There's water inside the quills. Look."

Susie squeezed one of the quills and some clear liquid seeped out. It didn't exactly look like water.

"I have to get ready for school."

Susie nodded. "Go on. The gutting isn't any big secret, anyway."

She plugged her transistor radio into the wall and adjusted the dial on some mournful song about a man whose girlfriend died and left him all alone. I could hear Susie's voice all the way upstairs as I pulled on my kneesocks and brushed my hair. "Honey, you died and left meeeeee . . . ," she sang above the clatter of the turkey roaster's lid, "but I'll see you by and by . . ."

I finally went in and woke up my mother and told her that Gus and I were going to be late for school. She struggled out of bed and said that her head hurt and then she put on her coat and got the keys to the car. By then the whole house was beginning to take on a strange, musky odor, like the underside of an old, rotting log, and Susie had begun vacuuming the living room rug with the radio turned even louder.

"Pee-eww," Gus said, making a face. "Why does she have to cook that thing in here?"

"Susie!" my mother shouted. "I'm taking the kids to school, but I'll be right back and we can start planning what to do with our first batch of quills."

Susie made an "okay" sign and went back to vacuuming. I had started to dread every morning because my mother always made us late and then insisted on dropping us right at the front door of school. It was bad enough that we arrived late and in a Mercedes instead of a pickup truck with a gun rack like most of the other kids, but also because everyone could look out and see my mother in her fur coat and nightgown. At recess people would ask Gus and me what was really wrong with our mother, anyway. At least now I could say that she had a business instead of just saying that she slept a lot and had a death wish.

But something changed that morning. All the way to school and for several mornings after that, we watched for roadkill along the shoulder. We now had a purpose, something to focus on. Part of the road followed along the shore of Lake Michigan and then back through the trees and the streets of houses. Usually there were at least a few dead animals, especially by the water. But we didn't find any porcupines that day or the next. In fact, we didn't find any porcupines all week. We saw a lot of crunched-up beer cans, a dead crow, and a brown support oxford that Gus begged my mother to let him keep. The shoe looked like it had been worn for a long time, and my mother yelled that it was germy and to get back in the car when Gus tried to pick it up. I thought about saying that dead animals were germier than old shoes, but I kept quiet.

Susie said it didn't matter that we didn't find any porcupines because she could supply all the carcasses my mother could handle, but I knew that my mother would have felt more useful if she had found her own. "It takes time," Susie told her after the first week. "You're new at this."

"I suppose so," my mother said. "But I really want this to work."

At first my mother was gung ho about the whole operation. The musky smell of boiling porcupine soon filled our house and clung to everything we wore. Susie arrived every morning with her burlap sack cradled in her arms and set to work dusting and vacuuming, the whole time singing above her jangling music as my mother tried to make sense of the porcupines in the kitchen.

After a couple of weeks, Susie was doing all the housework and even doing extra things like baking cookies and taking Gus and me for hikes in the woods. She'd tell us stories about these spirits that lived in the trees and how if we were very quiet and behaved ourselves we might actually hear them talking. I thought she was better than TV, but I could tell that Gus didn't buy most of the things she said.

Instead of making my mother feel better, all of this extra help seemed to give her more time to feel bad. She'd work with the quills for a little while, but then she'd spend the rest of the day lying on her back in her bedroom with all the shades pulled down, staring at the ceiling. One night, just as it was getting dark, she came out of her room and said, "Let's go for a drive!"

Her voice was happy, but her eyes looked tired and red, as if she'd been crying. Gus and I looked at each other over our plates of macaroni and cheese that Susie had left for our dinner. She'd even baked us corn bread in a special pan that made every piece come out looking like a little ear of corn.

"Okay," I said.

I didn't want to go but I didn't want to let my mother down, either, so we got in the car and started driving. At first it seemed like we weren't going anywhere in particular, but then my mother said, "I'm looking for a good straightaway at this point."

I wasn't sure what she was talking about, but it didn't sound good. When we turned onto Bester Road, which is more or less straight depending on which direction you're coming from, she pressed the buttons for all four windows and started accelerating until it seemed like we were going about a million miles an hour. She stuck her head out the window a little, and her hair tangled and whirled around her face.

"Mom!" Gus screamed from the backseat. "Slow down!"

I was scared, too. "Mom!" I yelled, but it was like she couldn't even hear me. She just stared straight ahead as the speedometer crept above a hundred. The light from the setting sun came slashing through the rows of pines lining the road like some giant flashbulb taking our picture over and over, and when I couldn't stand it anymore, I covered my face with my hands. But even when I shut my eyes tight, the light was like the sound of someone dragging a stick along a picket fence and I couldn't make it stop.

When my mother finally started to slow the car down, Gus was crying, and she was crying, too.

"I'm so sorry," she said, crumpling over the steering wheel.

The only reason I didn't start crying was because for a second I thought that we were probably all dead, and even when I opened my eyes and stared right into her face, I still wasn't completely sure.

After that night in the car, my mother began to sleep later and later, eventually even letting Susie drive us to school in the morning. Susie drove slow and would drop us off anywhere we wanted, so it was a pretty good deal in that way, but I worried about my mother waking up all alone in the house. I worried about what she might do, and I worried that if I wasn't there to wake her up that she might not wake up at all.

In the car Susie told us about how when she was a girl, she had to walk all the way from Cross Village to get to school, and if she was late the nuns at the Catholic school for orphans and Indian children would make her kneel on a cold stone floor and pray for an extra hour. "Once," she said, "I took the short-cut to get to school. I ran along by the water and the whole time I felt like someone was watching me. I felt the eyes of someone on the back of my neck. Someone who knew me well."

She peered at Gus in the rearview mirror.

"Who was it?" I bit my lip. "Who was watching you?"

"Who knows?" Susie muttered. "The water has its secrets."

I heard Gus stifling a yawn in the backseat. I could tell

that he didn't buy Susie's story at all. I believed her because she scared me a little and because even if she was a bad influence, she did a good job of taking my mind off my other bad influences.

By the end of the third week, my mother seemed to have gotten sick of quills. She made a few pairs of earrings and took them around to some of the tourist stores, but no one seemed very impressed. This depressed my mother even more. She had had high hopes for the porcupine business. Things really started to unravel when I slipped up and mentioned the business to Aunt Claire. I was at her house on bridge club day wearing a new fur vest that my mother had made for me out of some raccoon hides. When the earrings didn't go over very well, as a last-ditch effort she decided to branch out into clothing. Susie brought her some tanned raccoon and opossum hides to start with. The vest made me itch even when I wore it over a turtleneck, but I wanted my mother to believe that I loved it, so I had worn it three days in a row.

"What a *precious* little fur vest, Annie," Mrs. Minturn said, looking me up and down. "Wherever did you get it?"

I stared at Mrs. Minturn. "My mom made it for me."

"Is it rabbit fur?" Mrs. Minturn straightened her glasses.

"It's roadkill," I told her.

"I beg your pardon?" Mrs. Minturn said, setting down her cards.

"My mother is making clothing," I said, giving Mrs. Minturn a hard look. I hated her then.

"Well, how clever," Mrs. Minturn said, but I could tell that she didn't mean it at all.

L ater, after her bridge club guests had left, Aunt Claire took me aside and said, "I know what your mother is doing, Annie."

"What's my mother doing?" I asked.

Aunt Claire sighed. "Don't pretend." She looked very tired. "I'm making plans for your mother," she said, patting her hair. "I've talked to her about them."

"What?" I asked. "What kind of plans?"

"At some point, your mother is going to go away for a little while," she said. "She's agreed that she needs a little time away."

I started crying. It just seemed automatic, like I knew exactly what Aunt Claire was going to say even though I didn't.

"My mother needs to be with Gus and me," I said. "She needs to be with me."

"There, there," Aunt Claire said, putting her arm around my shoulder and giving me a hug. Her dress smelled like flowers and hair spray, not boiling porcupine. "It wouldn't be until the end of summer. This isn't an emergency, not exactly, and they don't have room until then. But even when she does go, it will only be for a little while and you and Gus can come and stay with me. Wouldn't you like that?"

"Where is she going?" I asked. My voice came out in a sort of sob.

Aunt Claire pulled a Kleenex out of her pocket and handed it to me.

"Here," she said. "Now blow your nose and try to calm down. It's a very nice facility in Minnesota. Silverlawns. Isn't that a pretty name? It's just like a country club. I have the brochure in the other room. I'll show you the picture and then you won't be so worried."

Aunt Claire went to get the brochure, and I blew my nose and tried to stop crying. I looked down at my raccoon vest and suddenly I could see where my mother had tried to make the different pieces of fur match up and the way every clumsy stitch stood out and it all seemed so shabby and hopeless. I started crying all over again.

"Now, now," Aunt Claire said, coming into the room. "Let's collect ourselves a bit. See?" she said, pointing to various pictures in the brochure. "Tennis and a pool. . . ."

The people in the pictures were all smiling like they were having the most wonderful time, like they'd never had a bad day in all their lives. I tried to imagine my mother in one of the pictures, but it didn't work.

"Now try not to worry yourself about this anymore. Put it out of your mind for now," Aunt Claire said. "I'll speak to Gus. He's a bit young to understand all of this but I'll try to explain in a way that he won't worry too much."

"Okay," I said, but what I really wanted was for someone to explain the whole thing to me.

That night, as my mother was reading Gus a bedtime story, she slumped over onto the floor and wouldn't move. Gus started crying and yelling that we should call an ambulance. I peered over and looked into my mother's face. Something about the way she was holding her mouth and the fact that she kept a tight grip on Gus's copy of *Treasure Island* let me know that this was only one more experiment. We shook her shoulders and tried to make her sit up, but she wouldn't open her eyes.

"If she doesn't move in two minutes, we'll call Aunt Claire," I told Gus. I said it loud enough so my mother was sure to hear even though she was slumped under the bed a little bit. Just as I was about to really do something, she moved.

"I wanted to see what you'd do if I died," she said, sitting up and rubbing her eyes. Then she started crying.

"It's okay." I put my arms around her. I wanted to tell her that it didn't work to pretend like that, that she couldn't disappear for a while and then come back, but I wasn't sure how to say it.

My mother walked slowly into her room and went to bed, but I lay awake most of the night thinking about what it would feel like to just want to die. I thought about what I read in my science book, how every person gets half of herself from her parents and the other half from her environment, and I wondered, as I studied the way the moon came through the spiny pine trees making patterns on my sheets, what part of me was my mother.

Early on Saturday morning, Susie Medicinehat came to say good-bye. Aunt Claire had talked to Susie and told her that my mother was going away for a little while at the end of the summer and that, in the meantime, she didn't need Susie's help.

I could tell Aunt Claire thought Susie was part of the problem with everything. I knew Susie was the best thing, the only good thing. I was sitting alone on the front porch when Susie came walking up the driveway. The truck that usually dropped her off was nowhere in sight and she looked like she had been walking for a long time. She sat down next to me without speaking.

"Hi," I said. "Do you want to talk to my mom?"

"Nope." She stared off at the trees. "I came to see you."

"Oh." I wasn't sure what she wanted from me. We were quiet for a minute.

"Here," Susie said finally and handed me a little package wrapped in a piece of a grocery sack. "Don't know what made me bring this over." She made it sound like an apology.

I opened it while she watched and inside, nestled on some shredded newspaper, was a quill box. Some of the quills on the lid had been dyed different colors and woven into a figure of a porcupine. The inside was made out of birch bark, and written across the bottom in crooked letters was the word *Annie*.

"Thank you." I turned the box in my hands. "It's really beautiful."

I knew that "beautiful" wasn't the right word, that it was something more complicated than that.

"You're welcome," Susie whispered. She put her hands in the pockets of her jeans and looked down like she was embarrassed.

We sat like that, the two of us alone together. I reached over and touched Susie's arm. She squeezed my hand once, hard and sure.

"Well, I've got to get going," she said, getting up and not looking at me.

"Are you positive you don't want to talk to my mom?" I asked her, but she was already walking down the driveway and waving good-bye, her back turned.

Two days after Susie left, my mother admitted that she might have to go away in the fall. "But only for a week," she told us. And that day she decided that she wanted to take Gus and me for a picnic on the beach. It was only early June and still not really beach weather, but she packed a big lunch and put on a pretty sundress and she seemed so hopeful and determined to make it a good time that there was no way we weren't going to go along with it. We drove up the shore until there weren't any houses, just trees and sand, and my mother kept saying, "Here? Shall we stop here?" but neither Gus nor I could bring ourselves to say yes.

Finally, my mother pulled in by a big dune and said, "This looks right. I think we've got the whole place to ourselves!" in a really cheerful voice. It made me sad that she was still trying so hard. We gathered up all the picnic stuff, but our hearts weren't in it and when my mother said, "It really is a gorgeous day!" I could tell that Gus was about to start crying.

We sat on the warm sand and ate our food watching the big waves change and shift with the wind, not talking much at all. After we were done eating, I looked for stones near the water, and Gus tried to build a sand castle. My mother lay on her back in the sun for a while and then went and stood with her feet in the water. I bent down to pick up a reddish stone, it looked like an agate, and when I glanced back at mother, she was gone.

That's when I saw her swimming out against the waves, saw her pink sundress balled up on the sand. "Mom!" I screamed, running out into the cold water until it came up to my waist. But she just kept swimming away, her white arms cutting into the sky.

"Mom!" Gus screamed. He started jumping up and down and waving his arms. "Please!" His voice was picked up and pulled away by the wind.

I started waving my arms. "Mom!" I yelled. "Mom! Mom!"

When she was out to where I could barely see her head, she turned and waved and then stopped for a minute. She swam back toward us and then stopped again. That was the first time I saw things the way she must have seen them. I saw Gus and me as two tiny figures jumping up and down on the sand. I saw the shore rising and falling with the waves, felt my arms floating outstretched. And when she had begun to swim to shore, to finally swim in, I felt the smooth sand shift out from under my feet. For a second, I let myself slip beneath, under the whole, blue deep.

NOW YOU LOVE ME

Outside of Wawa, we realized we could never stop. We could idle, we could pause; we could come to a slow roll or pull up short, engine coughing in some parking lot, while my mother ran in to get sodas or my brother, Gus, went to look for a restroom. But we could never really stop, dead and silent. The news hit us hard.

We had been avoiding the idea for miles, which was why, when Gus begged for souvenirs at Pancake Bay, my mother waited outside, letting the motor rumble low while I went in to help Gus pay for his plastic tomahawk and Indian beaded belt. It was also why, when we coasted up to the pump at the gas station in Sturgeon Falls, my mother kept one toe gunning the accelerator even as I filled the tank with the heavy silver nozzle, exhaust fumes lightening my head, the black hose twisting past my shorts and around my tennis shoes like a giant eel. It was why we had eaten our lunch doing seventy, all the windows rolled down, our hair tangling in our faces as we tried to chew. It was why, for hours, as we drove and drove, I stared down a river of flattened porcupines, bits of someone's windshield blown like bright confetti across the asphalt, broken green beer bottles, stunned blackbirds, tin cans accordioned one after the next, an endless ribbon of bad luck shouldering our path. It was why, by the time we hit Blind River and my mother announced cheerily, "I guess we'll just press on!" we acted as if this was our choice, we so wanted to believe. But by Wawa, we knew. There was no way to stop.

"This is a problem," my mother finally admitted at a scenic turnoff a few miles outside of town, "and I need to think."

For a minute, we were quiet. We watched Lake Superior while the car sputtered and twitched in park. Above the water, the sky was white. It had been one of the hottest Augusts on record in our part of northern Michigan where we'd started out, earlier that same day, and as we'd made our way into Canada, the clammy heat hadn't let up.

In the front seat, Gus fiddled with the radio, which only got AM stations. He passed over some polka music, then disco, and settled on people speaking French.

"La," he said, imitating. "Wee." He was six.

My mother sighed, running her fingers through her long hair. "It *is* a problem. But it certainly shouldn't ruin our nice vacation. I mean, it's not a problem we can't solve." She pressed the gas for a second and the car roared and shook.

"Yeah," Gus agreed. "It's nothing we can't solve."

I stuck my tongue out at the back of his small head. He was on his best behavior, wheedling for more souvenirs.

"Don't you think, Annie?" My mother peered at me in the rearview mirror, pushing her sunglasses up on her nose.

"How should I know?" I was tired; we'd been going for hours. I could tell that I sounded mad, but by then I didn't care. "What do I know about cars?"

That was the problem; none of us knew anything about cars. But even if we had, I wasn't sure it would have made much difference. The real problem was that we weren't driving a normal car: one with a key. The car, a big wood-paneled station wagon my mother had hot-wired right out of our neighbors', the Slocums', driveway back in Michigan, before the sun was even up, was stolen. "Borrowed," my mother called it, and where there should have been a key there was only an empty silver slot.

"Oh, *that*," I could imagine my mother saying if anyone had noticed the empty key slot and asked—the man at the border in Sault Ste. Marie who'd brushed us past with a wave, the woman who'd handed us our lunch at the drive-through window in Chapleau—"Oh, *that*." But no one had asked and now it made me nervous even to look at the empty place where the key should have been, like when you see the thin, loose shirt-sleeve of someone who's missing an arm and you glance away quick or keep your eyes low. Looking at the jumbled nest of rainbow-colored wires sagging beneath the dash was even worse. That's why I'd kept my eyes glued to the shoulder as we'd traveled north. Now I had no choice. I stared at the wires. They hung just under the dashboard key slot, knotted with my mother's own mixture of hope and beginner's luck.

"My main concern is this." My mother leaned over to poke at the tangled mess with the handle of Gus's tomahawk. "Of course"—she tugged a red wire and the car shuddered—"I'm afraid if we start monkeying around here we won't be able to get the thing going again. I don't exactly know how that part works."

I let out a long breath and rested my face in my hands.

"I know, I know," my mother said, still poking at the wires. "I wish I had a little more automobile knowledge. But let me tell you something, in movies they sure make all this hot-wiring look a lot harder than it really is. Wow, I mean, I got it right on my very first try! Maybe we're just lucky, but I ask you, how hard can it be? Not very. Now this stopping business . . ."

"But I ask you—" Gus started to repeat, so I grabbed a tuft of his hair and he quit.

My mother drummed her hands on the steering wheel and hummed. "I'm thinking," she told Gus and me even though no one had asked.

I turned and lay my head along the track of the opened passenger-side window and looked out across the turnoff lot. There were two other cars and a Winnebago, parked and silent. A family was having a picnic on the grass. In our noisy, stolen station wagon, my mother muttered to herself and pressed her forehead with both thumbs as she unfolded the Slocums' map of Ontario. Gus bobbed and clapped to the radio. I leaned back against the sticky seat. I was supposed to start fourth grade in two weeks.

"I vote we keep moving," my mother told us as she jammed the crumpled map under the front seat. The car lurched and growled. "For now at least." She shifted sideways and tried to smile at me, draping an arm across the headrest in back of Gus. "Because even though things aren't working out exactly as we'd hoped, I'm determined that we relax and enjoy ourselves." She blew her nose on a tissue she'd pulled from the box the Slocums kept stashed in the glove compartment. "That's what vacations are for."

A t first, we pretended that if we didn't talk about the station wagon it might go away. My mother was best at this. "Are you hungry?" she asked Gus and me just after the hot-wiring. "Because we can have breakfast anytime you want."

This was early, before we'd ever dreamed of how we might stop. It was still dark and we were driving fast, as if on fire, burning a trail up U.S. 75 North, our overnight bags pitched in the back, none of us turning around to see where we'd been: our empty house, our small sleeping town. The morning was opening blue over the station wagon's hood ornament and wind came piping through the air vents in a high-pitched squeal.

"We can have breakfast *before* we get into Canada," she said, lifting her fingers to her mouth to bite her nails, "or after. I think we should have it before, but it's up to you." She shrugged.

We were flying. The Michigan forests blurred into one big pine tree, and for a second the road seemed to widen and swallow us whole. I reached up and touched my mother's shoulder in the hazy dark of the car. Through the thin cotton of her shirt, I could feel bones, smooth and fragile, like the wing of some bird.

"Okay," my mother said. "We'll have breakfast after."

I pulled my hand back. Gus was chattering about how he wanted waffles, and my mother was letting the steering wheel float in her open hands. I tried to pretend that we were in our own car, taking a drive, but the seat of the station wagon was wide and unfamiliar. A pair of men's golf shoes rested on the floor and every time I bumped one of them with my foot, I remembered where we were. And even though it was scary and unbelievable, our being in the Slocums' car, it wasn't a complete surprise. All summer something had been building in my mother. It had started in May when she had agreed to go away to Silverlawns in the fall. That was when I first noticed the pacing. Sometimes, a long time after I was supposed to be asleep, I'd hear my mother downstairs walking, her slippers scuffing on the hardwood floors, back and forth, back and forth. It would last for hours. In the morning, her eyes would be pink and when she talked, one of her hands would sneak up to tug at her hair or you'd look down and see her foot tap-tapping fast. She was never still. She paced through June and all of July. By August it seemed as if she never slept, and it seemed as if it had always been like that.

The night before the hot-wiring, the sound of her footfalls was steady as the tick of the clock beside my bed. I didn't even notice it anymore. When I opened my eyes, my mother was hovering over me.

"I'm sorry," she said, patting me on the forehead. "I know it's early, but I wanted to get a jump on the day."

It was black in my room. I could make out Gus's small shape standing in the doorway, already dressed. "Here's a shirt," my mother said, helping me to sit up. I heard her opening my dresser drawers, unzipping my suitcase. "Come on," she told me when she turned back around to see that I hadn't budged. "Up, up."

"Where are we going?" I rubbed my eyes.

"We're going." My mother kept folding shorts and T-shirts into my bag.

"Where?" Through my window I could see the moon, spiderwebbed by tree branches.

My mother hefted my suitcase. "I have your bag all set. When you're ready, meet us on the front porch."

"Yeah," Gus shouted from the hall, "the front porch!"

Alone in my room, I couldn't think. I lay back down and shut my eyes. Then I felt around for my clothes, put on my shoes, and walked through our empty house. Outside, Gus was slouched next to our three suitcases on the front steps. All the stars were still out.

"Where's Mom?" I asked.

"She went to get the car." Gus stared at his feet, waiting. I peeked through the dark at the garage across the driveway, but I didn't see our car or my mother. Then I remembered. Our car was in being fixed. My mother had banged into a stop sign three days before, taking Gus and me to our swimming lessons, and the car had to be repaired.

"Which car?" I asked Gus. I didn't even want to know.

He pointed. The sound of an engine jerking to life came through the tall cedar hedge that divided our neighbors', the Slocums', yard from our own. I knew that Mr. and Mrs. Slocum were gone, in Europe for two weeks. Mr. Slocum was paying Gus and me a dollar a week to collect their mail. We listened to the Slocums' car. Neither one of us spoke. A second later my mother wheeled in the driveway. She leaned over to open the station wagon door. We didn't move.

"Come on," my mother said. "Get in."

Then we were on the highway, driving away, and none of it seemed real. In the dark, I tried to pretend. And all the way north—through Rudyard, Evergreen, Longlac—we didn't talk about the car; we watched the road. We kept moving, my mother driving faster than we could think. We kept going. We drove until we realized it was all we could do.

When we left the scenic turnoff without any plan of how to stop, I decided to quit pretending. My mother made excuses, she gave us ideas, but none of it made much sense. And by the time we'd backed the station wagon in a groaning U-turn around the lot—almost running over a KEEP OUR PROVINCE BEAUTIFUL. THANKS! trash barrel—and pointed the vehicle nose north toward Wawa, it had begun to rain.

"What next!" my mother laughed, groping for the windshield wiper controls.

"La!" Gus yelled, wound up from the sound of the rain beating down on the roof. "Go!"

I stayed silent, my arms crossed tight. My mother sensed my unhappiness all the way in the front seat, and as we sailed onto Highway 17 she took the turn in weather as an opportunity to give us a pep talk on the pluses of unplanned journeys. Part of traveling, my mother told us, was learning to expect the unexpected. "I'm not making any promises," she said, adjusting the rearview mirror, "but every trip has the potential to be an adventure.

"Adventure," she repeated, in case we'd missed it the first time.

I ignored her. The road was crowded by huge, jagged rocks and maple trees whose small leaves curled in like little fists. There weren't many other cars, which was good since we kept drifting over the center line.

My mother went on with her lecture, using the station wagon as an example. "Take this car, for instance," she told us, her voice loud and sure.

Gus had held on to his claim of the front passenger spot, and now he was nodding his head yes, buying the whole story, agreeing with the potential for adventure, the stolen car, all of it. At home, we never missed an episode of *Hawaii 5-0* or *Police Story*, so we knew some things about crime, but seeing Gus nod his head like that made me realize he was already gone. I kicked the back of his seat.

"This car is exactly the sort of thing I'm talking about," my mother continued, ignoring us. "I mean, it's a perfect example."

A red pickup truck tried to pass on the left. The driver raised his arm at us.

"I believe I'm driving the legal speed limit, my friend!" My mother shook her finger at the truck. "So as I was saying, this car wasn't part of the plan, but here we are." She paused. "Un-expectedly."

The rain fell hard, erasing our path.

My mother tried again. "You'd borrow someone's hat, right?" she asked us.

"Yes, I would," Gus said, even though I knew for a fact he'd never borrowed someone else's hat in his life.

"Well, it's no different," my mother said. "This car is a borrowed hat."

"Good," Gus said. "I like hats."

"Shut up," I told him. "You're in big trouble."

"Hey," my mother said. "No fighting. And if you need to express your anger, please find another way." She mumbled to herself and tried one last time. "This car is an opportunity," she told us, "an opportunity for the three of us to be together as a family."

"We're all in big trouble," I whispered, but it was drowned out by the car's snarl and roar as my mother gave it the gas. Then, as we came over the crest of a small hill, we passed a man waiting on the side of the road. For a second he was there, standing off the gravel shoulder in the tall weeds, clutching a piece of brown cardboard that read YELLOWKNIFE. He looked like the Marlboro man or the picture of the guy in my third-grade science book who discovered gravity, except younger. As we skidded by, he jerked out his thumb, leaned to one side, and tilted his neck. His body made the shape of a giant question mark.

"Now there's another good example," my mother said, nodding at the hitchhiker. "He has no car at all, it's raining, and he needs to be in Yellowknife. Was this part of his plan? Probably not!"

"Yellowknife," Gus said.

I flipped around on the seat and stared out the back window at the blue of the man's shirt. It got smaller and smaller until I could cover it with only my fingertip pressed against the water-beaded glass.

"Yes, Yellowknife," my mother went on. "That's basically at the North Pole. *Yellowknife.*" She made a clicking sound with her tongue. "So we're having a little car trouble and things aren't going exactly as we'd hoped. Big deal. Now if we had *his* problems, we could complain."

I turned back around. "We can't stop," I reminded her. "That's a big problem."

"Oh, Annie." My mother sighed. "You haven't listened to a word I've said."

Since there was nothing else to do, we decided to keep driving until dark, put off our trouble until Nipigon or Red Rock, but the minute we hit Wawa, just a few minutes up the road, Gus started whining for ice cream. My mother circled the two streets that made up the downtown until we found a Tasty Twirl with a drive-up window.

"Three vanillas," she told the woman.

"Chocolate!" Gus shouted. "With a banana on it!"

"He's tired," my mother said. "Just give us the vanilla."

"A banana!" Gus repeated. He crouched on the seat, cradling his tomahawk.

"Please." My mother dabbed at her forehead with one of the Slocums' tissues. She revved the engine while the woman made our cones.

"After this, no more sugar," my mother muttered, digging in her purse.

The rain had let up but it was still hot, and as we drove around looking for a place to idle while we ate, the soft ice cream melted down our wrists and dripped in slow glops on the seats. Gus didn't even try to save his.

"You're making a mess, young man," my mother scolded, but you could tell that her mind was on other things.

Near a cement replica of a giant Canada goose that guarded the entrance to the Wawa Chamber of Commerce building, we parked and got out. The place was deserted. The three of us stood looking at the snorting station wagon, the way you look at an elephant in a zoo.

"We need to regroup," my mother told us, pointing toward the building. "Please clean yourselves up a bit and use the restrooms."

I took my time getting the ice cream off my arms, and in the visitors' information booth set up in the hall, I read all the free brochures for canoe rides and camping sites, pretending for a minute that I was a normal tourist who might stop anywhere I wanted. When I finally came back outside, my mother was sitting on the rumbling hood of the car, talking. As I got closer I could see a man leaning under one of the goose's outstretched wings. I recognized the blue of his shirt. My mother was shaking her head at something he had just said, and when she saw me, she made a motion to come over. Gus had climbed up on the back of the statue and had his skinny legs wrapped around the huge bird's neck. His arms were still streaked like lit candles.

"This is Lincoln," my mother told me, pointing at the hitchhiker. She had her sunglasses back on even though there was no sun. "We passed him up the road and he still beat us here."

The hitchhiker smiled, moving from underneath the goose. "That's a fact. I was taking a little travel break under the bird here when you pulled in."

In person, Lincoln was taller than he'd seemed on the road. The backpack slung over his shoulder looked lumpy and soaked. His wet hair curled around his face and hung in his eyes. He was using his Yellowknife sign like a fan.

"This is as hot as it gets in Canada," he told us, giving the goose statue a friendly slap on the side as he fanned his face. "Which is why I'm headed north."

"That's nice," my mother said. "Have a good time."

"I've a cousin up there who's half Athabascan. We're going fishing. Up there, they fish with their bare hands. No hooks, no poles, nothing. It's worth the trip, believe me!" Lincoln laughed.

"Interesting," my mother told him.

"And you?" Lincoln asked. "Where to?"

"Around," my mother said. "Here and there."

"Shouldn't let your car idle too long, you know." Lincoln pointed at the station wagon. "Sounds like you've got some engine trouble, too."

"Oh well," my mother said. "Probably."

"Hear that ticking?" Lincoln put his finger to his lips. "You're running hot. If you want, I'll take a look."

"Oh, that's not necessary." My mother hopped down from the hood and stuffed her hands in her pockets. "Gus, climb off before you break something."

Gus poked at the goose's opened beak, pretending not to hear.

"Do you fix cars?" I asked Lincoln.

My mother coughed twice, loudly.

"I'm a mason by trade," Lincoln said, patting his chest. "But I tinker with autos on occasion. I certainly wouldn't mind—"

"It's nothing," my mother said. "Have fun in Yellowknife."

"Hey." Lincoln stopped fanning and pushed his cardboard sign under his arm. He held up both hands, palms out. "Whatever. Just thought I'd help a fellow traveler."

"We're fine," my mother said. "We're on vacation."

"Well then." Lincoln glanced in the driver's-side window and took a step away from the car. "Let me know if you change your mind."

"Okay," my mother told him. "I'll do that. Gus, get off the bird!"

"You're not headed to Yellowknife by any chance?" Lincoln flashed his sign.

"No, we're not." My mother opened the car door and signaled for Gus and me to get in.

"Thought you probably weren't." Lincoln sighed, scratching his chin. "So maybe I'll see you up the road."

By then the three of us were back in the station wagon and my mother was scanning the map, pushing her forehead with her thumb. Lincoln tapped on the window next to her, even though it was already halfway down. He bent so that his face was level with our own.

"Excuse me," he said. "You dropped this."

It was Gus's tomahawk. Lincoln handed it to my mother, the plastic blade cupped in his palm, the way they teach you to hold scissors. I followed his eyes to the dashboard.

"So okay," Lincoln said. "Aloha."

When we left Wawa, the sky had begun to get pink around the edges. We pushed north, following the shore of Lake Superior, the road growing dark and narrow as we made our way to Nipigon. The pavement was shiny from the rain, and I closed my eyes and thought about running and running. "Let's sing," my mother suggested. She felt around for the headlight button, and after they came on, you could see that there were only trees and trees and more rocks and water. The nest of colored wires rocked gently beneath the glowing dashboard. "Row, row, row your boat," she began. "Come on, you two!"

"We could have given him a ride," I told her, leaning into the front seat. "He knew about cars."

"Well." My mother gripped the steering wheel with both hands. "Let's not worry about that."

"I'm hungry," Gus said. "You should fix us dinner."

"Right," my mother said. "I'll do that."

"He knew," I told my mother.

"If you don't want to sing, I'm not interested." My mother stared straight ahead, not even glancing at me in the rearview mirror. "'Camptown Races,' you know that song?"

"It's dinnertime!" Gus shouted.

"You're absolutely right," my mother said. "That's our number one priority."

But there weren't any restaurants, or gas stations, hardly even any other cars. "The next town we come to, we'll get something to eat," my mother promised. "And some gasoline. This thing gobbles gas. It certainly wasn't built for distances."

The station wagon was howling by then—the sound of someone having a good, long cry—and for the next few miles, my mother didn't try to give us another pep talk about unexpected travel or make us try to think of the words to "Camptown Races." White moths and June bugs swirled in our headlights above puddles in the road. After what seemed like an hour, maybe more, we passed Pukaskwa Provincial Park and a place called Dog Lake, which was really only one closed-up bait shop and a big sign advertising shotgun shells.

"We might not make it to Nipigon," my mother told us, crinkling the map over the steering wheel, "but I see that we should hit Marathon at any second."

A half hour later at the one self-serve gas station in town, my mother showed Gus how to keep his foot pressed on the accelerator and she got out to pump. While she stood in a circle of fluorescent light, swatting at mosquitoes, I peered over the headrest at Gus. "You could be in big, big trouble," I told him, narrowing my eyes. "Trouble with the law."

"What?" he asked. He was hunched up trying to reach the gas pedal, and his Indian beaded belt was pulled too tight around the waist of his shorts, making them wrinkle at his hips like a paper sack. Dried ice cream ringed the edges of his lips and zigzagged across the front of his shirt. His face caught the greenish glow of the gas station sign just so. "What?" he asked again.

I sat back and kicked at one of Mr. Slocum's golf shoes resting on the floor.

"What?" Gus stared at me over the seat.

"Nothing," I told him.

We watched my mother finish pumping the gas, and after she'd paid the man inside and gotten back into the car, she took a minute to review our situation.

"Look, I've been thinking," she told us, licking a finger and smoothing it over one eyebrow. "I know things look bad *right now* and believe me, it's not how I'd pictured it. But what do you say we try to keep ourselves together until a reasonable solution presents itself?" She poked at the wires and shook her head sadly.

"Okay," Gus and I mumbled.

"Thank you," my mother told us in a weak voice. "You really are being good sports about this."

We headed down Main Street to find a restaurant where we could keep an eye on the car from our table. It was easy to decide since there were only two restaurants in Marathon and one was really a bar and didn't have any windows.

"No, I don't think so," my mother said, passing it by. "That makes me nervous."

We ended up having dinner at a place called EAT. It had a big parking lot and windows by every booth. While we waited for our food, we took turns cupping our hands to the dark window to peer at the station wagon rumbling just outside. Gus had ordered the deluxe fried chicken special, and when it came he chewed with his mouth open. I tried to be hungry but nothing tasted right. My mother took a couple of bites and then sat looking down into her lap. By then it was as if something had turned in all of us and we were slipping and sliding, moving and falling, even when we were sitting still.

On the way out, when our waitress told us to have a good evening, my mother made a brushing motion in the air. "I've had it," she said, to no one in particular.

It seemed like things were as bad as they could get, but

when we got to the parking lot, Lincoln was standing in the shadows near the station wagon. The Yellowknife sign was sticking out of the top of his backpack, and it looked like he'd combed his hair and maybe even shaved. He gave us a big smile.

"Good God," my mother muttered.

"We meet again," he said. "Got dropped off up the road and I couldn't help but notice your vehicle as I was walking past. Still having some car trouble, I guess."

My mother frowned and clutched at her purse.

"Well," Lincoln said, kicking at the pavement. "Let me know if you want me to take a look at the thing. I wouldn't mind a bit. In fact, it'd make me feel useful."

He threw his arms wide like he wanted to give us all a hug.

"Thank you, no," my mother told him. "But we appreciate your offer."

We stood there, the four of us beneath the stars, listening to the car.

"You're a complicated woman," Lincoln said suddenly, turning to my mother.

"Whatever." My mother sniffed.

Lincoln fake coughed and looked at the ground. He patted the side of the station wagon. "In my opinion, strictly a guess, mind you, you shouldn't even be driving the thing. That's without my actually examining the vehicle. That's what I'd say."

"Thanks for the tip," my mother told him. "*Get in,*" she whispered.

Gus and I climbed into the station wagon and my mother slammed the door. We were jammed in the front, side by side by side. The colored wires rested on my knee.

"I'll be around," Lincoln said, as my mother was putting the car in reverse. He trotted next to us as we backed in a slow curve around the parking lot. "There's no reason for you to be afraid of me. I can see that you're a single parent, and I want to say that I'm an honest businessman. I'm a homeowner. I even know CPR!" He broke into a run as we pulled out on the street. "Hey!" he shouted after us. "I'm only thinking of the children! You should let me help you!"

"I'm finished with men!" my mother yelled at the windshield. "Forever!"

Lincoln stopped running and dropped farther and farther away from the car.

"Boy," my mother said after we'd gone a couple of blocks. "That guy is really starting to get on my nerves. What a day. I think we'd better just rest here tonight and try to get our strength back and decide what to do in the morning."

Gus nodded, but I didn't move. I couldn't get the picture of Lincoln running next to our car out of my head—the way he'd tried to smile and touch the wood-paneled side just before we left him. He was the only person who wanted to help us and my mother had almost run him over.

"You don't even have to say it," my mother admitted as she scanned the road for a motel. "This is our worst vacation ever."

That night we stayed in a cabin that had a stuffed squirrel mounted on a table in the spot where a TV would usually sit.

"I *hate* this." Gus jumped up and down on the cot the cabin manager had set up for him in the corner, waving his tomahawk and leaving small gray footprints on the sheets. The cabin had real log walls and a shower with a slanted tin floor. Through the open window you could hear the hum of mosquitoes and the endless droning of the station wagon.

"Please behave yourself," my mother told Gus as she unpacked our overnight bags. "I wish we had a TV, too. I wish we had a lot of things. I wish . . . ," she started to say. She stopped unpacking and went and sat on the edge of one of the twin beds. I was already lying on the other bed, and when she began to speak I propped a pillow behind my neck and listened. Her words came out like the story of our lives and they made me want to close my eyes, but I couldn't.

"For once," she said, keeping her head bowed, "I really wanted to get something right. I wanted to do something nice, something normal." She paused, turning to look out through the dark window. "I've tried, but I always seem to mess things up somehow." She pulled one of the Slocums' tissues from her pants pocket and wiped her nose. "Some days, I've been very sad. I apologize for worrying you."

"We weren't worried," Gus told her. He sat on his cot and dangled his feet above a burned spot in the rug.

"Please." My mother held up one hand. "Let me continue. I'm sure I haven't been the best parent, that's what I'm trying to tell you. These things happen. But I love you more than anything, and I wanted to do something good before I have to go away. Then one day I thought to myself, what my children need is a vacation. That's what I thought this morning, actually, at about four A.M. My children need a vacation! An honest-togoodness vacation. They need to run and laugh and skip in the sand. A vacation." She blew her nose. "It sounds silly now." She gestured to the bedside lamp, which was shaped like a teepee. "But that's what I thought."

"I like this vacation," Gus told her.

"Me, too." I didn't know what else to say.

"I love you," my mother told us. "I meant well. I wanted you to know."

She sniffled and reached out to pat the stuffed squirrel. "This is someone's idea of decorating." She pulled her hand back and looked down at her lap. "Oh, the world," she sighed. "The world, the world."

When I woke up, everything was silent. Gus was still asleep but my mother was sitting up, the ugly orange bedspread pulled to her chin. Her face was smooth and unworried. She looked as if she had been expecting this.

"Hear that?" I asked her. She nodded. We slipped out of bed and walked in our pajamas and bare feet to the station wagon. On the picnic table next to the car there was a note written on a piece of brown cardboard held down by a rock. *"Hey,"* it began. *"You need to touch the green one to the blue one to get it going. These are your ignition wires. You can unhook them again any time you want to stop. Make sure that you stay far away from the yellow and the orange. These are dangerous and pack a wallop. Touch the ignition wires once and keep your hands on the plastic-coated parts only."* The note went on to give specific directions about each wire and what it did. At the end it said: *"I care about you or else I*

wouldn't have bothered. Keep this in mind. Your fellow traveler, Lincoln."
When I turned the note over, I saw the letters Y-E-L-L.

"Well, he found us." My mother opened the station wagon door, looked in, and then slammed it shut. "But at least now we can stop."

We stood staring off down the road. We waited, leaning against the hood. It was obvious that he was long gone. After a while, we went back inside and took showers and got dressed. When we were packed and the car was loaded, we climbed in and my mother held Lincoln's note across her knees and went to work. The station wagon howled to life.

"We can do anything you want," my mother told us when we'd pulled up to the highway. "North or south?"

"North," I said. It seemed like the only answer.

My mother steered, keeping Lake Superior on our left. I rolled down the back window and let my arm drag in the wind. There were lots of other travelers—a bus, two campers, a long line of cars, but no hitchhikers. In Red Rock, when we stopped for breakfast, my mother used Lincoln's note again and shut the car off. "That was easy," she told us, sounding disappointed. And even though it was nice to be able to eat slowly, to sit in one place and not worry, every few bites I'd look up and catch my mother straining her neck to glance out at the station wagon. When she was looking down, I did the same thing. It was no use.

After we'd finished breakfast and gotten back on Highway 17, we headed north toward Thunder Bay for one more look. We watched the side of the road, anxious around every curve, but for miles there was nothing, only a few tin cans and a dead raccoon. Then, on a flat stretch that ran along the water, I saw someone up ahead. He was standing on the lake side, pitching rocks down the sloping, weedy shoulder and across the beach. When he heard the car, he stepped back toward the road and held out his sign. Now it said OWKNIFE. He hadn't even tried to make it look right. After we'd pulled over and gotten out, he told us he thought it was good enough to get him where he was going. "People will know what I mean," he said.

He went back to throwing rocks in the water, choosing each one carefully from a pile he'd set up on his backpack. Some of them skipped a few times. Some sank right away. He didn't seem all that happy to see us. We stood on the shoulder, watching him throw. A truck sped past and sounded its horn.

"We wanted to thank you," my mother told him, "for fixing our car."

"Right," Lincoln said, keeping his back to us. He threw more rocks, first with his left hand, then with his right.

"No, really," my mother said. "You went out of your way for us."

Lincoln went on pitching, putting his whole body into each toss.

"I mean it," my mother told him.

"Oh, *now* you love me!" Lincoln laughed, but he said it as if he was mad.

"We're going home," my mother said. "But we wanted to thank you first."

"You're welcome!" Lincoln shouted above the waves. "Have a nice day!"

"Okay, kids, I think we'd better go." My mother pushed us toward the station wagon.

"No, wait," Lincoln said, turning fast. "Not yet."

Since I was standing nearest, it was me he got when he reached out and grabbed. He gripped my arm tightly, his strong fingers digging into my skin, and for a second I let myself be pulled toward him and down onto the beach. I don't know how long he held me. When my mother screamed, he let go.

"Stop it!" she spit at him. "What do you think you're doing?"

Lincoln put one finger to his lips. "Watch this," he told us.

He picked up a rock from his pile. It was flat, the shape of a saucer, smooth and white. He drew his arm back and sent it out over the water. The rock skipped about a hundred times, again and again—more than I could count, more than I could see. I got up from the sand and ran. Then we were back in the station wagon and my mother was crying hard. She did a squealing U-turn and headed south, flooring the engine. I sat in the back, shivering. I didn't feel like crying. And the whole way home, while my mother said she was sorry over and over, and tried to think of a story to tell the Slocums, everyone, about our trip, I kept putting my hand against my heart. It fluttered and jumped just under my T-shirt. I listened with my fingers. It made the sound of that white rock, hopping across the water. "Wait, wait, wait," it said. "Stop, stop, stop."

SURPRISE

Gus folded himself inside our mother's open suitcase. His skinny legs dangled over one side and his tennis shoes dragged across the tangled bedspread. He looked like a person in a too-small rubber raft, floating nowhere, kicking in circles. I sat on the floor, listening to the rain hitting the windows and watching him. "You know you're not going," I said, after a minute, "so don't even try."

Gus didn't answer, but one of his hands reached up slowly, his fingers feeling in the air. He grabbed the buckled leather strap dangling from the top of the suitcase and pulled it down, closing it over his body.

"And even if you were going," I told him, "that's a really stupid idea."

Our mother was supposed to be packing for Silverlawns, but instead she was standing in her closet, yanking clothes from hangers and throwing them onto a big pile in the center of the room. The pile had summer dresses and thick sweaters, pale cotton blouses and a heavy coat. She had been doing this for half an hour. All the shirtsleeves and pant legs wrapped around and around one another, caught and held tight in one huge swirl.

"I'm wondering about the weather," my mother said from behind the half-opened door. "That's one of my problems right now."

She threw two more skirts on the pile and then came out carrying a pair of blue gloves and a wool scarf. She laid the gloves and scarf on top of the rest of the clothes and went and sat on the edge of the bed next to the closed suitcase. I got up and sat beside her.

"Gus," she said, patting one of Gus's ankles. "I want to talk to you for a minute."

"No." Gus's voice was tiny and muffled from inside the suitcase, as if someone was holding a hand over his mouth.

"Gus, please." My mother lifted the boxy lid of the suitcase and peeked in at him. "Talk to me for a minute, okay? It's important." She knocked on the suitcase. "Come out, come out, wherever you are."

Gus pushed open the top and sat up. He hooked his elbows over the stiff leather edges and frowned at my mother. His nose was running and I could tell that he had been crying.

"We all need to cooperate a little bit," my mother told him. He shook his head no and scrunched back down farther into the suitcase.

"Yes. And sometimes we have to do things we don't want to do because, in the long run, it's for the best. Of course I don't want to go," my mother said. "But I know that I have to."

"Why," Gus said. He made it sound not like a question.

My mother retied Gus's tennis shoe, which had come

undone. She was staring at the pile of her clothes. "I have to go," she said, "and I've explained it to you as best I can."

"You're not coming back," Gus said then. It was what I might have said, some other time, or if I had thought of it.

"Now, you know that's absolutely not true. I'm coming back before you even have a chance to miss me."

My mother reached over and tried to tickle Gus on the stomach. Then she stood to lift him. When Gus was out of the suitcase he hunched, crossing his arms over his chest, and wouldn't look at anyone. My mother sighed and sat again. Now the three of us were together, next to the empty suitcase, there on the rumpled bed.

"What if you just didn't go?" I asked.

"Oh, sweetie, that's not an option," my mother said, checking her watch. "Apparently."

"Listen!" Gus shouted and we all stopped, quiet, listening to the rain falling through the late afternoon. There was no other sound.

"What is it?" my mother asked, turning to put her face close to his.

"I heard someone downstairs," he said. "I heard someone walking around downstairs."

"You did?" My mother tucked her hair behind her ears and cocked her head to one side. "I didn't hear a thing."

"Please go and see." Gus kept his arms crossed and didn't move. "I heard someone."

My mother let out a long breath and patted Gus's head. She smiled at him and held his cheeks in her hands. "All right, but I really think you're imagining this."

I followed my mother down the stairs while Gus stayed behind. We walked from room to room, but there was nothing to see; everything was in its place. My mother shrugged and opened the front door. She left it like that and we went out onto the porch and down onto the front walk.

Outside, it was almost sunny but raining at the same time. I looked up at the sky and back at the house. Gus was in the window of our mother's bedroom. He had pushed it open.

"There's nothing here!" my mother called to him. "All clear!"

Gus disappeared for a second. When he was at the window again, he pushed it up even farther. Then he was fiddling with something too small to see.

Afterward, he wouldn't explain how he had known the exact way to unlatch the screen.

"Gus!" my mother yelled, his name catching in her throat. "Don't move! Don't move!"

But it was us who didn't move, my mother and me; we stayed perfectly still. We were standing in the yard, looking up, not moving at all, when one of her blue gloves came floating down from above.

THIS BEAUTIFUL DAY

Don't go to Goodwill, don't go there. Don't go even if someone takes your hand in his small, sweaty one and begs please. Say no.

That was what I repeated in my mind, that fall, when it was already too late and we had gone to Goodwill and our lives were different and worse because of its charity. I always understood perfectly what was over and finished. Still, I liked to try to remind myself how not to let things happen again.

It started the day after our mother left for Silverlawns, the Saturday we played miniature golf all morning at the place out by the highway, taking turns hitting tiny white balls into the alligator's and hippo's wide-open mouths. The miniature golf was Aunt Claire's idea. She was keeping Gus and me until our mother could come home again. No one would say exactly how long that might be. The day before when we had driven my mother to the airport, Aunt Claire at the wheel, me in the front next to her, Gus and my mother in the back, my mother had said three weeks. "Four, tops," she'd added, looking down at the thick stack of magazines in her lap, the ones she had brought to read on the plane. "Possibly five," she'd whispered then, tracing her finger along the edge of one of the magazines.

"Paige," Aunt Claire had said, making my mother's name sound like a whole sentence. She'd shaken her head quickly and kept her eyes on the road. "Let's not."

"You can think of it this way," my mother had said then to Gus and me, ignoring Aunt Claire. "I'll be back in time to take you trick-or-treating. Halloween."

"Halloween," Gus had repeated, softly. "Halloween."

I knew my mother didn't know how long, that three weeks was just a guess. Mostly, I'd been trying not to imagine. I knew Aunt Claire was trying hard to keep us from imagining, too. It was why we'd been bowling the night before, had pancakes for breakfast; it was why we were playing miniature golf. Still, all that Saturday morning, between putts, I stared down at the fake grass or up at the September sky, rolling flat and gray above us, and tried to see my mother at Silverlawns with her suitcases and her magazines. I imagined. When I looked at Gus, I knew he was doing it, too.

It made it tough to concentrate on the game. The object was to get the big smiling animals to swallow everything. There were twelve of them, animals, and that morning we were taking them in no particular order. We'd almost made it past the pink elephant with the bobbing trunk before Gus started bawling. He had that kind of crying that could also sound like a laugh, like hiccups or a giggle caught far in the back of his throat. Then the yowling would start and that sounded like an electric can opener pressed to On for a long time. He'd sway and rock when he really got going. If you didn't know him very well, you could believe that he was having a good time.

Aunt Claire was turned, taking her putt at the elephant, so she wasn't paying attention when Gus started in crying. "This certainly is different," she was saying just then. It was something she had said four times already that morning. She dipped her body at the waist and kept her stubby club gripped hard in both hands while she aimed at the elephant's legs. "But I think I'm getting the hang of it," she added.

Out of the corner of my eye, I watched Gus wander over to the ninth hole—a blue whale with a cement water spout. Even from a few feet away, I could hear him hiccuping fast and loud.

While Aunt Claire was practice swinging, I crouched down next to him. "Don't even," I said, but I knew it was already too late. Once he got started, the day was ruined. The two of us stayed like that for a second while Gus made sharp coughing noises and used the sleeve of his windbreaker like a Kleenex. He rested his cheek against the whale's smooth side and began the can opener thing.

"Luckily, there aren't a lot of people to hear you," I said.

I pointed at the only other people who had also been playing, an old man and a shorter woman with long brown hair. Now they were walking past the squatty red windmill with the spinning spokes and out toward the deserted parking lot. The old man had his arm around the woman's waist. I wondered what it would be like to get in their car with them and go wherever they were going.

"I think I'll run and ask them if they want a new son," I told

Gus, twirling my golf club between my palms. I poked him in the foot with the flat hitting part.

"Get away from me," he said, blowing his nose.

"I wish I could," I said. "Boy, do I ever."

Lately, I'd been trying to hurt his feelings for no reason. It was like a new hobby. While I was thinking of what to say next, a fat raindrop fell out of nowhere and made a dull smack right between the whale's two big scary eyes. Gus stopped moaning long enough to put up his hood, tying the strings in a tight knot under his chin. Then he went back to making a steady blubbering noise. I put up my hood, too, and we both watched Aunt Claire.

"Will you look at that!" she yelled to us. She had taken her putt, and now she was trying to pick up her ball from where the elephant's trunk had knocked it into one of the little plastic pine trees that lined the pathway. She clucked her tongue. "I'm quite certain this place is rigged."

She walked over, holding the white ball up and peering at it. She pulled her reading glasses from the pocket of her corduroy skirt and squinted. Next, she stared at us sitting beside the whale.

"Are you weeping?" she asked Gus.

"Yes," I told her.

"Annie, I'm asking Gus," she said. She got down on her knees on the scratchy grass and put one hand on his shoulder. I saw how her heels slipped out of the backs of her loafers. She had only ever taken care of us for a week or two at the most. I could tell that she was nervous we might do something she couldn't handle. With Gus, she used a slow, clear voice, the kind people have when they talk to a pet. "*Gus,* dear, are you *hurt?*"

"No, he's not," I said. "But it's going to be tough to get him to stop." I cupped my hand out and caught a few heavy drops. "Also, it's raining," I pointed out.

Aunt Claire studied the sky. The three of us were quiet while a truck hummed past on the highway in the distance.

"See here," Aunt Claire told Gus, taking his hands in hers and frowning. "Nothing terrible has happened. Everything is just fine. There's absolutely nothing to upset you so."

She handed Gus a white hankie she'd pulled from somewhere. "What is it I can do?" she asked me while Gus used the handkerchief. I didn't answer and instead tried to concentrate on a chip of paint peeling off the neck of a nearby spotted giraffe.

Aunt Claire helped Gus to his feet and I stood, too. When she hugged us both close, I turned my head to see the low black clouds. The wind had picked up and now it was blowing rain across the whole miniature golf course. The animals were shiny with water. Wet, they looked like statues or something more beautiful than what they were before.

"I think you're hungry, that's all," Aunt Claire told Gus finally, letting us go. "I think it's time for lunch."

Gus was still hiccup-crying, but he nodded his head yes. Once I'd seen him eat a whole baby-sized cheeseburger, howling between every bite, so I knew he could eat.

Aunt Claire smoothed the short hair around her ears. "Can we have a nice calm meal?" she asked. She closed her eyes. "Wait, don't answer that."

The three of us made our way single file over the soggy plastic lawn. After we'd returned our clubs to the man at the ticket counter and gotten into the car, Aunt Claire added something.

"At times in your life, you simply must be patient. And soon enough, everything sorts itself out again."

"When?" I asked.

"When?" Aunt Claire repeated. She started the car and turned on the windshield wipers. "You know what I mean."

We drove to Darrow's Drive-In and ate in the car with the windows rolled up against the rain. By then Gus was still crying on and off, but also stuffing french fries into his mouth three at a time.

"This is good, Claire," he said from the backseat.

"Excuse me?" Aunt Claire looked at him in the rearview mirror.

"He does that now," I explained, taking a sip of my milk shake. "He's copying TV." A month before, Gus and I had seen a show about a boy who goes to college to become a doctor when he's eight. Since then Gus, like the TV boy, had been calling adults by their first names.

"Well, I don't think we can have that sort of thing," Aunt Claire corrected.

She dabbed at the corners of her mouth with a Darrow's napkin. Then she unsnapped her purse and took out a tube of rose-colored lipstick and put it on, staring straight ahead.

When we were finished eating, a girl with an apron tied over her jeans came and took the tray from where it was hooked over the window.

"Fine, fine," Aunt Claire said to herself.

She put the car in reverse and we backed out of the parking

space. It was after we'd pulled out of Darrow's and we were halfway up the street that Gus spotted the Goodwill sign. In our town, there was really only one main road, so it wasn't like we hadn't seen the sign a million times before.

"Stop!" Gus yelled, pointing.

"Gussy, you don't want anything in there," Aunt Claire told him.

"Please," Gus said. I could hear that he was about to start crying again. He put one of his sticky hands on the top of Aunt Claire's hairdo and patted. "Please!"

Aunt Claire sighed and turned into the lot next to Goodwill. When she'd shut off the car, she stared at Gus. "What is it?"

"I need to go in here." He folded his arms over his chest.

Aunt Claire gave me a look, but I shrugged. "Once he has an idea," I told her.

We all got out and went into the Goodwill store. It was dark inside, but I could see that there were racks and racks of dresses and shirts in all sorts of bright patterns. A lady was talking loud on the telephone behind the cash register. "Fact is, you'd think he'd learned that lesson," she was saying. She smiled at Aunt Claire.

Everything smelled like ashtrays. Along one wall by the shoes was a row of old TV sets. One was turned on to *Gunsmoke*. Gus and I walked over and stood in front of the screen, watching as two men in cowboy hats kicked their horses in the ribs to get away fast. Aunt Claire picked up a pair of sparkly high heels and put them back down.

"Have you seen enough?" she asked Gus.

He pretended he hadn't heard and ducked under a bunch of winter coats. I saw Aunt Claire bite her lip.

"Whatever it is," I said, "it's probably best just to buy it right now."

Aunt Claire nodded. When we found Gus again, he was at the very back of the store, holding what looked like some sort of big dead animal.

"I'll rake leaves and pay you back," he told Aunt Claire.

"Ha," I said. "That's pretty funny."

Aunt Claire reached out and touched the fur. She put on her glasses and pulled at the tag in the fuzzy neck part. "'Junior male large costume,'" she read aloud.

"Isn't that a cute little suit?" the lady called from behind the counter, covering the phone's mouthpiece with her palm. "Someone brought that by only yesterday."

Gus stepped back and held the furry suit tight against his body. It was eight sizes too big. Behind him on the shelf were the hands and the gorilla head part, staring at us. "This is what I would like to have," Gus said. "Claire."

Aunt Claire bent and whispered. I leaned in to hear. "This is a charity," she told Gus. Her breath smelled like wintergreen Life Savers. "Do you understand that this is a store for people who need things but who cannot truly afford to buy them?"

"Good." Gus smiled.

"Oh, for God's sake," Aunt Claire muttered. She squinted at the price tag on the monkey costume. I'd never heard her swear before.

At the cash register Aunt Claire put down a twenty-dollar bill, but the woman wouldn't take it. "Nope," she yawned. "Not going to charge you for this one."

"I simply insist," Aunt Claire told her.

"It's a fine costume; he'll get some wear out of it. But see this ugly rip down the whole side?" The woman pointed in the fur with her frosty fingernail. "Can't take your money. Why don't you pick out some work boots or a lamp? Then I'd charge you."

"I insist," Aunt Claire said again. She clicked her purse. Her face was pink.

"Go on." The woman laughed. "We like to help out where we can. That's why we're here."

"Thank you," Gus said, staring at the woman's nametag, "Maryjane."

When we were back in the car and on the way home, Aunt Claire warned Gus in the rearview mirror. "I'm quite upset right now, young man. I won't abide any more bad behavior. Of course this is a difficult time. But there's still no excuse for ill manners. You must try to keep an even keel. And you're not to wear that until Halloween. Understood?"

Gus sat silent in the backseat, holding the gorilla suit in a wadded-up grocery bag on his lap. Someone had crossed out the name A & P with a Magic Marker on the front of the sack and written GOODWILL in capital letters in its place.

I threw my arm over the headrest and poked the bag with my thumb. Gus slapped me away. "Get ready to rake some leaves," I told him.

"Annie, be still," Aunt Claire said. "And no more of this crying business today. Anyone," she added, fluffing her hairdo back from where Gus had pushed it flat earlier. "My heart can't take it."

No one talked after that. It had stopped raining and the sun was making the trees look the color of bonfires. In Aunt Claire's driveway, we stepped around the puddles and fallen maple leaves. While Aunt Claire went inside to rest, Gus and I sat on the front porch and stared out at the street, which was much busier than the one where we lived.

"What do you think you're going to do with that thing, anyway?"

Gus shook his head, clutching the bag on his knees. "It's mine," he said. "I will love it."

Then he did what we were all trying not to do, which was bring up our mother and Silverlawns.

"I was wondering if they have miniature golf there," he said after a minute. "Mom likes miniature golf."

"No, she doesn't." I picked up a red maple leaf from one of the steps and pressed it to my palm. "She hates miniature golf. Lots of people hate miniature golf."

"I bet they have an indoor swimming pool with a slide." He hugged his grocery sack.

"It's not like that," I said, but Gus had turned to look at a man in the yard next door. The man was pushing a shovel into the ground with the heel of his boot, making a hole. We watched the digging for a while.

"Don't think you're going to dress like an ape and go out in public," I told Gus.

"If they don't have miniature golf and they don't have a pool, what do they do all day?" Gus stared down at his tennis shoes and then back at the man next door.

Before our mother had gone, she'd tried to explain things to us. It was as if Gus had forgotten all of it on purpose. Truthfully, when I thought hard, I understood most of it and not very much; both at the same time. A blue jay screamed from high in a tree.

"It's almost like a hospital," I said. "She reads magazines. You know."

"Okay." He nodded. "I know."

I closed one eye and squinted at the clouds, like the insides of a torn pillow, flying past above us.

"Just please don't try to be weird." I tugged at the cuffs of my jacket.

"I won't," Gus promised, but he didn't sound sure.

"I'm serious," I told him. "It's so important."

That night the phone rang late. I got out of bed and crept to the top of the stairs to listen. I could tell from Aunt Claire's low voice that it was my mother.

"Yes," Aunt Claire said. "They're just fine."

She was quiet for a minute.

"No," she answered to some question. "You should take it easy and not think. That's what you're there for. Absolutely. Whatever he recommends."

Gus tiptoed up behind me in the dark and sat by my feet.

"If the man says he's a doctor, then I would assume that he's a doctor." Aunt Claire sighed from below. A chair scraped on the wood floor. Everything was silent. "Paige, you're there to get well, not to think," Aunt Claire said. "Good, you do that. I will tell them. Yes. Good night."

"Good night," I repeated to Gus.

"Good night!" he shouted to Aunt Claire.

"Back to bed, please!" she called to us in a tired voice. "It's very late."

The next morning, Aunt Claire and I were already in the kitchen having breakfast when Gus came downstairs. He was in the suit. He stood in the doorway for a second, not moving, his small hairy body outlined by the window's pale sunlight. On a filmstrip once, I had seen a picture of the creature that came between monkeys and real human men. This was how Gus looked. Aunt Claire sucked in her breath the way you do when you're about to swim underwater for a long time. She took a sip of orange juice from one of the little juice glasses she'd set at each of our places and put her hand on her forehead.

"Remember what we agreed?" she asked him. "That is your Halloween costume."

Gus pulled out one of the high-backed chairs and sat next to me. He had on the body part of the suit, half-zipped up the back, and also the scowling gorilla face mask and the rubber-fingered paws—the complete outfit. Up close, it wasn't exactly realistic. His fur smelled like cigarettes and Vicks VapoRub, and besides the big rip down the side there were egg-shaped patches on both elbows where all the fuzz had been worn down to a stubble. You could imagine that whoever had worn the suit before had leaned hard on a table for a long time, smoking.

"I bet you think you look great," I told him.

Gus pretended not to hear. He reached out and wrapped his gorilla fingers around a toast corner and began shoving it in through his rubber gorilla mouth, pointy end first. A few crumbs fell and caught in the hairs on his chest. Next, he hunched his shoulders low over his bowl of cornflakes and made loud smacking noises.

Aunt Claire and I watched him trying to eat.

"Take your head off, please," she said, after a minute. "We need to have a family meeting."

Gus stopped with the cornflakes and sat still. Aunt Claire smoothed the edge of her place mat, making it flat. She coughed, once. I could hear the grandfather clock ticking down the hall in the living room. When the phone rang, Aunt Claire said, "We'll continue this discussion in a moment."

After Aunt Claire had gone to get the telephone, I grabbed one of Gus's brown furry wrists and pulled.

"Let go!" His voice was lower, as if he was talking from behind a shut door.

I squeezed his arm until he yelped. Then I yanked a tuft of hair near his monkey ear and pinched. He jumped up and stood behind his chair, panting. That was when I noticed the way the suit hung and bunched over his skinny body like a leftover hand-me-down from some bigger, grown-up gorilla. I quit.

"That was Mim Ford," Aunt Claire told us, coming back into the kitchen. "They need a fourth in bridge this afternoon. Do you think we can find something to keep you children occupied for an hour or so while I visit with my friends?"

She picked up her coffee cup and went over to the counter. "What would you ordinarily do on a Sunday?"

"Not this," I said, pointing at Gus, who was still standing

behind his chair. He had stopped panting and was staring at me, or at least it seemed like that. It was hard to say.

"You shouldn't be the one staring," I told him.

"Okay, okay. We'll find something fun for you two to do," Aunt Claire said. She closed her eyes for a second. "Annie dear, help me with the dishes and then we can make our plans." She faced Gus. "And I've decided that you may wear your costume. But only inside the house and only if you've finished your homework."

"He doesn't get much homework," I told Aunt Claire. "In first grade they don't."

Gus nodded his gorilla head.

"Well then," Aunt Claire said. "That's settled."

While Aunt Claire and I were putting plates and spoons in the sink, I heard the front door open and close. Aunt Claire hummed while she moved her hands in the soapy water. After a minute, the sound of a car driving past and honking loud came through the open window by the kitchen table. While I was drying a glass, someone drove by, yelling. There was more tooting and screaming.

"What is that racket?" Aunt Claire asked me.

She wiped her hands on a blue-and-white dish towel and went to look. I stood next to her.

"Oh," she said, craning her neck and drumming her fingers on the window screen, "this won't do at all."

Gus was under the oak tree, near the mailbox. He had gotten a rake from the garage and was pulling it across the lawn. From a distance, it really did look like a tiny ape was doing the yard work.

"Gussy!" Aunt Claire shouted. "Come inside!"

Gus waved but kept raking. A pickup truck went by slowly, swerving near the curb.

"He heard you," I said. "But don't plan on anything. I think he's trying to be helpful, though." It was true that Gus was actually raking the leaves into a pile.

"He could give someone a heart attack, that's my concern," Aunt Claire told me. "I myself am not feeling well. All these . . ." She looked at her watch. "Unexpected little surprises."

She was quiet for what seemed like forever. Someone yelled, "Hey, monkey boy!" For a minute, there weren't any cars. Gus was bent over, picking up sticks.

"That was your mother who called last night," Aunt Claire said. "She wanted to say hello and that she misses you, but that everything is going very well. She'll call us again when she knows something new."

"Okay," I told her, nodding and wishing that I could have been the one to talk to my mother. As Aunt Claire and I watched Gus, I thought of my mother and wondered what she was doing right then, right at that exact moment while we were there, doing what we were doing.

"Why is it that I never had any children of my own?" Aunt Claire asked suddenly. I picked at a loose piece of yarn in the hem of my sweater. It was one of those questions you could never know the answer to, so you don't even guess. "I don't know."

Aunt Claire thought for a minute. "Funny, I forgot what I was going to say," she told me. "But it was something."

That afternoon Aunt Claire drove us to the movie theater for the G-rated bargain children's matinee.

"This is a lovely film," she said, opening her purse and reaching over to hand me a ten-dollar bill. "You'll love all the singing and dancing."

"We don't go to movies alone, Claire," Gus told her. After the raking, he had refused to take off the suit, except for the head, and no one had stopped him. Now he was sitting in the front seat next to Aunt Claire, kicking his tennis shoes back and forth. From the back, I stared at his skinny neck sticking up from the big furry rest of his body.

"Nonsense," Aunt Claire said. "When I was your age, I went to movies all the time with my little friends. Here is the phone number of where I will be playing bridge." She slipped me a yellow piece of paper with some numbers on it. "And I'll be right here to pick you up when it's over. Annie will make sure you're fine."

"No, I won't." I crossed my arms and stared out the car window at the other people going into the theater. They were all families or mothers and their children, laughing and having fun.

"You most certainly will." Aunt Claire clicked her purse shut. From the way she said it, I could tell she was already getting sick of babysitting us.

"Now, I'll be back to get you in exactly one hour and forty-five minutes. Popcorn but no candy, and Annie take your brother's hand so that he doesn't wander off. Go, go," she said. "I'll wait to see that you're safely inside."

On the sidewalk, I grabbed Gus's clammy monkey fingers and we went in to get our tickets. We were the last people in line. I tried not to see if anyone was staring while we waited.

"It ain't Halloween for a month," the woman in the booth told us when we finally got to the front of the line. She passed me the change through the hole in the glass. "What are you supposed to be anyway?" She smiled at Gus.

"It's from Goodwill," I said. "It's a gorilla suit without the head."

"Cute." The woman smiled again, showing her teeth.

"Corrine," Gus said.

The woman stared down at the tag pinned to the front of her shirt. She looked up slowly. "He's pretty young to be calling folks by their names like that." She leaned forward and narrowed her eyes. "God, that's spooky."

"He saw it on TV." I tightened my grip on Gus, who was pulling toward the candy counter.

"Huh," she said, not smiling. "Still spooky."

By the time we'd gotten our large popcorns and Milk Duds and jujubes and found seats in the front row, the movie had already started. It was about a lady who lived with nuns and then went to live with a family of six children and a father. The children sang songs standing in one straight row.

"I'd like to do that," Gus said in a loud voice. He chewed his popcorn with his mouth open and rubbed his salty monkey gloves down his front.

"Why is that little boy wearing a fur coat?" the man sitting behind us whispered.

I kept eating my Milk Duds, pretending I didn't hear. When the children in the movie went on a picnic on a mountain, singing, Gus stood and walked back up the aisle. He was gone for a while, two whole songs, and when he came back he said that we had to leave.

"No way," I told him. "It's just at the good part." On the screen, one of the girls and her boyfriend were jumping over things and spinning and hopping in a rainstorm.

"Yes," Gus said right in my ear. That close, it was hard not to notice the cigarette smoke and VapoRub smell of his fur. "I need to go now."

"Wait." I watched the boyfriend trying to kiss the girl. The girl stretched her beautiful arms far away from the boyfriend. Gus crouched on his seat. Beside me in the dark, he started to hiccup-cough.

"Here," I said, passing him my napkin, which was slick with popcorn grease. Now the girl was running away in the rain. When I peered back at Gus, I could see that he had his face covered with both hands. "Okay, we'll go," I told him. "But we're going to be in big trouble."

Gus wiped his nose on his fuzzy sleeve. When we walked past the ticket booth it was empty. Out on the street, no cars were parked in front and no one was driving past. I didn't know what time it was, but I thought it was probably going to be a while until Aunt Claire came to pick us up.

"Why did you have to do that?" I stood a few feet from Gus so if anyone were to see us standing there, it would be hard to tell that we were actually together.

He shrugged and rubbed his eyes. "Two boys in the bath-room . . ." he started. He kicked at a piece of loose sidewalk with the toe of his tennis shoe. "Tried to hit me."

"They hit you?" I thought of all the boys it could have been, second graders like Charlie Swiss or Andy Bergy. There were lots of people who would hit someone dressed in a minia-ture gorilla suit.

"They grabbed me." Gus touched the matted, ripped part of his furry coat. "Here. But I got away."

"That's good," I said. "You got away."

"They didn't hurt me," he added. "I mean, they didn't get to. Yet." He sniffed.

It was only late afternoon, but the sunlight had already almost disappeared, leaving long purple shadows. Somewhere someone was burning leaves and that smell was everywhere. Inside my pocket, I crumpled the phone number Aunt Claire had given me. I walked out and stared up and down the street. I didn't know what I was looking for. The ice cream parlor and the gas station, all of the stores looked flat and not real, like the paper kind in a pop-up book.

"I'm ready to go home," Gus said.

"We can walk," I told him. "It's not that far." In truth, it was a long walk to Aunt Claire's house, but I wasn't sure of where else to go. I took Gus's hand now on purpose. We started up the street, moving slowly because the heavy legs of Gus's suit dragged over his ankles and made him shuffle. After we'd passed the grocery store and the Laundromat, he stopped to rest.

"Look." He pointed. We were right in front of Goodwill.

We pressed our faces to the gritty window and peeked in. In the darkness, I could see a rack of snowsuits and a sewing machine, but that was all.

"Charity is love," Gus said, slow and clear. "Goodwill. Believe in the power of work." He raised one fur-covered rubber gorilla paw at a big sign posted just inside the door, on one of the side walls. "I was reading that," he told me.

"Well, don't. You can't really read very well, anyway." I stared at the black letters on the sign, the words exactly as Gus had said. "You did get that mostly right," I admitted, "but I'm not sure how. You're lucky, I guess." I pulled him and we started walking again.

"I like charity," he whispered.

"You don't even know what that is." I tugged at his arm to keep him moving. The downtown ended suddenly, by the lumberyard, and the rows of houses began.

"I still like it," Gus said after a minute, squeezing my hand tighter as we stepped over a crack in the glittering sidewalk. A chained dog barked as we passed. Gus repeated the word softly, like the name of a friend: "Charity."

The trees were moving over our heads like huge, colorful bouquets. Gus started to hum, and as we walked past all of the quiet houses, I imagined them filled with families, filled with people sitting down at long tables to eat on white plates, filled with people reading books or watching TV, taking naps, singing a song in the kitchen. I didn't have to see to know that they were there, those families, behind every door.

Then we did something I couldn't explain. Instead of walking on to Aunt Claire's big house, four more blocks, we turned without saying anything and went down our own street, the road to the house we usually lived in with our mother, our home. We both knew exactly where we were going. It was there at the end, after six other houses, all already boarded up for the season, the summer people gone. It had been only three days since we'd been away, but the lawn was already ankle deep in dry, dead leaves no one had raked. The curtains in the upstairs windows were pulled tight. On the porch, I jiggled the front door handle, but it was locked. A few leaves had blown flat against the screen, and stayed, pressed like little hands. I brushed them down.

"Here we are," Gus said, hugging his shoulders and hopping on one foot. "But no one's home."

We walked down off the porch and circled the house. In the back, the lake was smooth and silvery gray. Along by the hedge, all the flowers in their beds were dried and brown, their drooping stalks making whistling sounds in the breeze. At the end of summer, our mother had stopped watering them.

It was getting cold and I pushed my hands in my jacket pockets, touching the paper with the phone number that Aunt Claire had given me. I kept my head down. Seeing our house like that, from the outside and in secret, felt like a mistake, like opening a door and accidentally catching someone changing their clothes. For a second I stared up at one of the curtained windows, my own bedroom, the way a stranger might. I tried to remember all the hundreds of times I had stood up there and looked down through the branches of the trees. It was too hard to imagine. I looked down at my shoes, kicking free a path in the orange and red leaves that kept drifting, one by one, from the sky.

"On Halloween I'm going to put my pumpkin—" Gus started to say when we came around to the front steps again.

"It might not be Halloween," I said. "We might not be here then."

"Yes." Gus pointed up at the top porch step. "On Halloween, when Mom gets back, I'm going to put my pumpkin right there."

"I doubt it," I said. We both watched our dark house. "Okay, you can," I told him. "Let's go."

I turned and marched, pulling Gus across the lawn as he stumbled through the leaves. He whined and tried to break free, but I held his furry arm and we walked, fast, away, Gus dragging, me almost running, until we were back on Main Street, next to the big white United Methodist church. When we stopped, Gus was panting. I tried to reach for his hand, but he twisted away from me, and all the way back downtown he followed at a distance, a few steps behind.

At the end of the street, I could see Aunt Claire's car parked in front of the movie theater. When we got closer, I saw her standing by the theater doors, talking with the woman who had been in the ticket booth. Aunt Claire was gesturing with her palm held flat, a couple of feet off the ground, the way you show how tall something is. Her purse was sitting on the sidewalk.

"See," the woman said when she spotted me with Gus. "There's the young monkey and his sister now. Told you they'd show right up."

"Where were you? The movie's been out for twenty minutes!" Aunt Claire covered her mouth. Her hand was shaking. I could tell she was angry, but her voice was also afraid. She crouched next to Gus and hugged him tight around his saggy waist.

"We just went for a walk," I said. "Down the street. Gus was feeling sick."

"I feel fine, Claire!" Gus shouted into her ear. He gave me a dirty look.

"Oh, I never should have let you go to the movie alone. How foolish, really." Aunt Claire patted me all over, on my chest and my back, the way I'd seen her plump a pillow. She studied me through her glasses. "I just assumed . . ."

"Hey, don't be so tough on yourself," the ticket lady told Aunt Claire. "Kids are here all the time by themselves. Working mothers and whatnot." She pulled a pack of cigarettes from a big pocket in her cardigan sweater and lit one with a lighter. "I'd send my own kids, but they can't walk out on their own yet. One's ten months and the other's two." The woman smiled through the smoke she was blowing out her nose. "But when they can."

"Thank you for all your help," Aunt Claire told the woman, standing and pushing Gus and me toward the car. "It is certainly much appreciated."

"I didn't do a thing," the woman said, waving. "Come again soon!"

On the ride back to her house, Aunt Claire took off her glasses and cleared her throat. "I don't think we have to mention this to anyone," she told us.

"Mention what?" I asked, putting my head back against the seat. When I shut my eyes I saw red leaves falling from the sky.

"Your wandering away from the movie like that." Aunt Claire paused. "It was my mistake. It was a misjudgment on my part. Like the miniature golf. But it's over. Okay?" she asked.

"Okay," I said, opening my eyes. "But who would we mention it to?"

"I don't know," she said. "Anyone." She gripped the steering wheel with both hands. "I apologize for not doing better with all of this."

"It's not you. It's him." I turned to look at Gus. "I just wish he'd stop wearing that." I pointed my thumb toward the backseat where Gus was. He'd taken the little pink comb out of Aunt Claire's purse and was using it to get all the fur on his arms to puff. "Then everything would be fine," I told Aunt Claire.

"Your sister has a concern," Aunt Claire said, turning to glance at Gus, "and from now on, we will try to honor each other's worries." She furrowed her forehead. "Wishes. Each other's wishes."

That night when I walked past the guest room where Gus was, on my way to brush my teeth, I saw him sitting on the floor trying to pull off his tennis shoes without untying them. He was still in the monkey suit and had slumped down against a chair, facing the window, his head bent to one side. From the back, he looked like some kind of broken toy. When I came from the bathroom a couple of minutes later, he was already in bed, his fuzzy black shoulders half covered by a quilt, his plastic gorilla hands folded neatly over his chest. The hall light fell in a bright streak across his face, and I could see that his eyes were wide open.

"You can't wear that to school tomorrow," I told him, stopping in the doorway.

"I know," he said. He sat up a little. "What I was wondering was if I could call Mom and talk to her about it."

Aunt Claire was downstairs washing dishes. I could hear her turning the faucet on and off, on and off. "Right now?" I asked.

I went into the room and sat on edge of the bed.

"Yes. Now."

From below, there was the sound of a metal pot falling to the floor. "I don't think so," I said, tracing one of the little calico squares on the quilt with my finger. "But I know she'll call when she has some news. When she has something new to tell us."

It was a cool night and the window was open a crack. I shivered in my nightgown. "I know what she'd say right now, though," I told Gus.

"What?" He blinked his eyes slowly.

"She'd say—" I started to say, but then I stopped because there was a loud crash, like a ball being thrown through a window.

"Oh, for mercy's sake!" Aunt Claire hollered.

Gus and I listened.

"Claire dropped a plate," he yawned. "She drops lots of things."

"You should try to be normal," I told Gus when it was quiet again. "That's what Mom would say."

It was a lie. I knew our mother would never say anything like that. It was what everyone said to her.

Gus shut his eyes. Then, without looking, there in the yellow half-light, he pulled off his gorilla gloves and put them on the nightstand. They lay there, the fingers still tightly crisscrossed. Underneath, Gus's real hands were pale and dimpled, the way hands look when they've been in a bathtub for a long time. He pretended to snore.

"It's a start," I said, poking him. "I'm almost proud of you."

"Okay," Gus said from the middle of his fake sleep. "But I'm not proud of you."

It was like a new beginning, and after that day we all started trying harder. All week, Aunt Claire drove us to school, and she was always parked and waiting to pick us up when we were through at three, sitting in the car reading thick paperback novels or doing crossword puzzles, her glasses pushed down on her nose. And all week, Gus wore jeans and Shetland sweaters, striped T-shirts and corduroy pants. He only put on the gorilla suit to watch *Police Story* or *Hawaii 5-0* on TV and once to play in the yard. The rest of the time, he dressed like a regular person. I tried to be nice to him, to make it my new hobby, and on Wednesday when our mother called to say that she was almost fine and that she might be home even before Halloween, I was ready to believe her.

"What do you think of that?" I asked Gus. I meant about our mother coming home in a couple of weeks. We were standing in the hallway where we'd just hung up the phone. Gus and I had on our windbreakers to go for a bike ride. Gus nodded, but he didn't say that he was happy or excited. It was the fifth of October, but a warm, clear day, and the windows were open to the breeze, the white curtains moving like bedsheets on a line. Aunt Claire was baking sugar cookies in the kitchen.

"Wait here," he told me.

I stood by the door and waited while Gus went upstairs. When he came back down, he was carrying the wadded-up grocery sack.

"I'm ready," he said.

I stared at the sack and started to say something, but Gus put his finger to his lips. "Please," he whispered.

We called to Aunt Claire, who told us not to go far and to be back in half an hour. Outside, on our bicycles, riding under a tunnel of orange and gold trees, the sky that perfect blue and the grocery bag in Gus's basket, I asked him why.

"I've decided I'd rather be a pirate," he said. "Or a doctor."

I nodded my head yes. "Good," I told him. "I'm glad."

We rode the rest of the way to Goodwill without talking, pedaling down the winding road to Main Street, past the lumberyard, the Spot Bar, and the hardware store. We parked our bicycles in front of Goodwill, next to a pickup truck. Inside, a man with a beard was looking at a baby stroller. He pushed it sideways and leaned on it hard. Gus and I stood by the wall, watching one of the black-and-white TVs and waiting until the man had paid for the stroller and left. The woman behind the counter was a different one from the last time.

"Is Maryjane here?" Gus asked, reaching up to put the grocery sack next to the cash register.

"Why no, she's not," the woman said, surprised.

She had blond hair done up in a bun and wide arms. She looked exactly like the picture of the lady on the pancake mix.

"Maryjane only works on Saturdays and Tuesdays. Is there something I can help you with?" Her voice was like birds chirping.

"We got this gorilla suit here a few days ago," I explained. "And now we're bringing it back."

"Is there something wrong with it?" the woman asked.

She opened the sack and lay the suit flat on the counter. The three of us stared at all that matted brown fur. She reached in and pulled out the head part and the gloves. "Hmmm . . .," she murmured. "I do see the rip."

"It was like that before," I told her. "We're bringing it back because we're done with it. He changed his mind."

"I've decided to be a doctor," Gus told her, "or a clown."

"Oh, I see. Halloween!" The woman smiled. "You're returning it so that someone else might wear it as a costume. How generous of you! Then you're bringing this to us as a donation?" She blinked, her blue eyes big and watery.

"What?" Gus's mouth made an O shape.

"A donation," she said, writing something on a pad. "You are donating this back?"

Gus stared up at her.

"A charitable donation?"

Gus frowned.

"Charity?" She bit her pen.

Now Gus nodded. "Okay, but what does that mean?" he

asked. By then the woman was rustling with the sack. I started to count the high stacks of baby clothes piled on the shelves: fourteen. I counted the pairs of tiny, scuffed shoes: twelve. Then I counted the toasters: nine. Then the cowboy boots: six. I stopped and watched the woman again.

"Would you like a receipt? It's a deduction on your taxes. Your parents will surely want one."

"Charity." Gus half-whispered this.

"We don't need a receipt," I said. "I'm pretty sure."

"Judy." Gus stood on his tiptoes, reading her nametag. "Tell me, okay?"

Judy stopped and squinted at Gus. She put down her pen. Then she unpinned her nametag and set it on the counter. "I've always hated wearing that thing," she told us. "Now, tell you what, honey?" she asked. Her voice was slower, not at all like birds chirping.

"Charity," Gus said. "What it means."

"Well, that's a good question. That's not the kind of question our customers usually ask. More like, 'Why do you want five whole bucks for this old coat?'" She laughed. Then she touched her forehead and thought. "Let's see. Well, I guess what it really means is kindness towards others. When a person truly needs something, someone is there to give it to him."

"Always?" Gus asked.

"Usually," Judy said. "That's how it works here. Supposedly."

The three of us were silent. It was hot and shadowed and dusty in the store. Gus and I had been gone too long. We should have left right then, gone back to Aunt Claire. I turned and looked out the big window at the street outside, at the one maple tree, its glowing leaves blowing and twisting in the wind, in that afternoon so bright it seemed on fire.

"I'll think of what I need," Gus was saying.

"That's all you have to do." Judy rubbed her temples. A streak of sunlight by her elbow showed the millions of particles floating in the air. I knew something. I could touch the dented toasters, the baby shoes worn gray, the work shirts with somebody else's name sewn above the pocket, all those things no one wanted but someone would take.

"Like this," Judy told us, closing her eyes and clasping her rough hands over the crumpled grocery sack. "Bow your heads. We will now give thanks for this beautiful day."

FEVER

When I opened one eye my mother was sitting on the end of the bed. She had on a turtleneck sweater the color of a stop sign and was holding a wrapped present on her lap. Bright sun filled the room, as if it were morning, or the afternoon of a perfect day, I wasn't sure which one. I had had the flu since Tuesday and now when I tried to lift my arms they felt as light and stiff as cardboard cutouts, not real parts of my body. When I breathed in fast, my heart fluttered against the sheet like a paper valentine heart, like something you could reach out and crumple with one hand. I tried not breathing. I blinked. "You're back," I told my mother, but later I realized that I probably hadn't said those words out loud.

"Hey," she whispered, smiling and tapping my foot through the blankets and quilt Aunt Claire had piled there the night before. She leaned over and kissed me on the cheek, three times. She was still clutching the present.

I shut my eyes again for a second. Her sweater was the kind of red that made it hurt to look. Then I sat up and propped my head against the pillow. I was in the guest room at Aunt Claire's house, and my mother was sitting on the end of my bed. I hadn't seen her for five weeks and two days.

"How are you feeling?" she asked.

"I don't know," I said after a minute. I stared at her. Except for the sweater, which was new, she looked exactly the same.

"That's good," my mother said, brushing the hair from my forehead with her cool fingers. "I mean, if you're not sure how you feel, that probably shows you're actually feeling better." She took the glass of ginger ale with the bent straw from the bedside table and held it for me to take a sip. "That's one thing I've learned."

"Really?" I swallowed the warm soda, letting the sharp bubbles slide down my throat. I could hear Gus yelling in the yard below through the half-opened window.

"Really." She smiled and rubbed my shoulders. "I missed you so much I can't even say."

"How would I know if I wasn't feeling better?" I asked. It seemed important.

My mother had set the present where my knees would be and was adjusting the blue ribbon on top of the box. There were tiny smudges of purple under her eyes and the ring she always wore was missing. Now I could see that she didn't look exactly the same at all, but different in ways you could only notice up close.

"How would I know?" I asked again.

"Look, this is for you," she said. She pushed the box toward me on the quilt and waited while I opened it. Inside, under all the white tissue paper, was a seashell, pearly and smooth and cold. I turned it over, tracing its spirals. It was heavier than it looked. "Thanks," I told her.

"I saw this and I thought *Annie.*" My mother took the shell from my hands and held it to her ear like a telephone. She closed her eyes. "You don't find many seashells in Minnesota," she said. She still had her eyes shut, listening.

"Where did you get it?"

My mother didn't say anything. She moved closer and pressed the shell to my ear to hear the ocean, the waves trapped inside. In my other ear I could hear Aunt Claire walking across the kitchen floor downstairs, fixing breakfast or fixing lunch, I still wasn't sure. The imaginary ocean roared. My face was hot, the room was too bright, and when I reached up and touched my mother's hand, she moved the shell away and gently placed it on the extra pillow.

"Unfortunately, I didn't find it on the beach," my mother told me. She picked at a fraying spot on the cuff of her jeans.

I nodded and she gave me another sip of warm ginger ale. She pushed the tissue paper back into the box and set it on the table next to a teaspoon resting on a saucer. She was smiling at me. "I can't stop looking at you," she said.

"Where did you get it?" I asked again.

"Oh, I bought it in a store. We went shopping on Wednesdays and Saturdays. That was the schedule. Ordinarily." She felt my forehead. "You've been running a little fever, but now I think you're cooler. Much cooler. You just need to rest."

I swallowed. I could see my mother's watch when she turned her wrist. "I didn't know what time it was," I said. "I was wondering if it was morning." I coughed. "Am I okay?"

"It's twelve thirty," she told me, "and you're absolutely fine." She tucked the quilt under my chin and pretended to look serious. "Okay. Let's make sure. Who's the president?" she asked.

"Ford."

"You're right!" She tickled me. "Where do you live?"

"Three thirty-one Harbor Street."

"Count the number of fingers I'm holding up."

She waved her open palm. We were laughing then.

"And what's your name?"

"Annie Elizabeth Child." I stopped giggling and what I had been trying to do for weeks happened. I could picture my mother someplace else. I could imagine her saying her own name, hear her answering those same questions, for real. I turned my head and looked at the seashell on the white pillowcase, lying there like a thing that had just washed up from the sheets.

My mother was nodding yes and still smiling. "One hundred percent positively okay," she said. She started to get off the bed, but I leaned forward and grabbed her arm. "I'm going to let you get some sleep now," she told me, patting my back. "I'll be right downstairs with Aunt Claire. And later, if you're feeling a bit stronger, we'll go home." She fluffed the pillow under my neck. "How does that sound?"

"I'm glad," I said. "I'm really glad you're here."

"I'm right here." She was in the doorway. "Close your eyes."

When I woke up again, the room was almost dark. Someone had moved the teaspoon and saucer, the crumpled Kleenex, from the bedside table. I felt around on the flat pillowcase. The seashell was gone.

Later, I ate a bowl of chicken broth from a tray Aunt Claire had set on my lap. It was night and my mother was sitting in a straight-backed chair she'd pulled next to the bed. She had been asking me about school. I bit the edge of a pale cracker and felt the grains of salt on my tongue. We were alone in the room. I said what I had been thinking of for a long time. "What was it like?"

She didn't look down at her hands. She didn't move. "I'm not sure how to answer that," she told me. "What would you like to know?"

"What it was like." I let the cracker dissolve in my mouth.

My mother touched her chin. "What it was like. It was a good place for a while. And some days it was boring. And all days I missed you and Gus." She unfolded the cloth napkin Aunt Claire had put on the tray and laid it so the broth wouldn't drip on my nightgown. "Everyone was very friendly. Well, most people, anyway. There really wasn't much good or bad, I suppose. It wasn't one way or another."

I finished the cracker and the chicken broth while my mother watched. She said a few things about the food there, a doctor, the books she read, but she didn't seem very interested. "In lots of ways it reminded me of a very nice hotel." She checked her fingernails.

I wiped my mouth with the napkin. I thought she was done with everything she would ever tell me about Silverlawns. The bedside lamp had been catching our shadows on the far wall, the two of us sitting like that, talking and not talking; our bodies copied once, beyond us. I wanted it to be morning so I could put on my coat and run outside and breathe. I felt my forehead and it was almost cold.

My mother leaned forward, her voice low. "If I said it was like being in heaven when you really only wanted to be on regular old planet Earth, would you know what I meant?"

I nodded, watching our shadows, but I didn't know.

"Mom!" Gus called from the bottom of the stairs. "Come see this!"

"That was what it was like," my mother told me, getting up from her chair. She lifted the tray from my lap.

I said: "Heaven."

"Maybe that isn't the right word." My mother tilted her head, listening. "Now that I hear someone else say it."

LIGHT

Shepherd Nash drove us out into the middle of a field. The sound of tall, dry grass rushing beneath the truck was like cupping a seashell close to my ear, that sound of wave after invisible wave disappearing to a place I would never see. Wildflowers folded, long weeds crackled and bent. He had something secret to tell us, and when we had driven up onto a little hill with a view of a falling-down barn and then the big lake in the distance, he shut off the engine and pulled a small, navy blue velvet box from his electrician's shirt pocket. Inside was a ring. The diamond on it was the size of a big grain of sand or maybe two big grains of sand, pushed together.

"It took me a really long time to choose this one," Shepherd told Gus and me, waving the box close to our eyes so we could get a good look. We were both in the wide front seat beside him. Gus was in the middle and our feet were resting on the lid of one of Shepherd's toolboxes, our wadded-up jackets, and a book I was reading about a girl and her horses. Shepherd had stopped for us as we were walking home from school and brought us here. We hadn't seen him for weeks or months, not since our mother had decided not to date him anymore. Now, instead of looking at the diamond ring, I stared at Shepherd, his stubbly beard, the tear on his sleeve, his scarred and bruised knuckles. Some of the scars were pale and looked like they were from a long time before, and some looked red and new, like they were made last week. I wondered what Shepherd had done to get them. The velvet box looked strange in his cut-up hand.

"You'd be surprised at what they try to pass off as fine jewelry," Shepherd said.

He shook his head slowly from side to side as if that made him sad. Then he took the ring from its thin velvet slot and held it up to the light. I could see that the band part wasn't a perfect circle, but stretched or melted somehow, more like the outline of a not quite full moon.

"Annie, Gus. Give me your honest opinion." Shepherd pinched the ring tightly between his thumb and first finger and held his breath.

"It's so beautiful," Gus said, reaching out to touch the sand-grain stone.

"I think it might be a little bit small," I told Shepherd. "But I'm not sure."

He frowned. "My affection is huge."

"That's good." I shifted my feet on the toolbox and thought about what that meant.

The three of us looked at the ring for a while as Shepherd turned it this way and that and scratched his beard. Under the hood, the truck engine went on ticking like a half-broken alarm clock, and the late afternoon sun coming through the smeary truck windows made everything go the color of honey. The diamond threw tiny rainbows on the front of Shepherd's shirt. He kissed the ring, once, loudly. Gus poked me in the ribs and started to say the word *why* but Shepherd interrupted.

"I am a man in love!" he bellowed into the windshield. Then he sneezed. "Hay fever," he said, blowing his nose on a dirty bandanna that had been lying on the dashboard. He rolled down the driver's-side window. "Please excuse me. I'm feeling pretty crazy right now." He put his forehead on the steering wheel and shut his eyes.

"I understand," Gus told him. He patted Shepherd's shoulder.

"Love just ties you up in knots! Knots!" Shepherd said, sitting up again fast. "I am a human pretzel. A human pretzel in love! Half the time I can't even remember my name." He held the misshapen ring on his flat palm.

"Shepherd," Gus said.

"What?" Shepherd asked, yanking at a handful of his own hair and sighing.

"Your name," Gus said.

"He doesn't mean that he really forgot his name," I told Gus, rolling down the window on my side of the truck. The air was almost cold and smelled like hay and all the flowers we had run over. It was the end of fall. I watched a black-and-white cow that had wandered up to a fence nearby. The cow stretched its neck over the barbed wire and yawned, sticking out its long tongue. "Sometimes you're so stupid," I said to Gus.

"The thing is, you can't understand it until it happens to you," Shepherd went on, ignoring both of us. "You cannot understand the true depth of my emotions. It's like when you see a movie about two people who fall in love and you think, 'No sir, that's not how it feels,' because the people are acting like they just got run over by a damn freight train. And then it happens to you. Bam! Out of nowhere! Well, I'm here to tell you that I'm starring in that movie, and I've been run over by that train."

"Okay," Gus said, nodding. "You've been run over by a train." He pulled a smashed piece of Bazooka bubble gum from his pants pocket and offered it to Shepherd. "I was saving this, but you can have it," Gus said. "It's grape flavor."

"Thanks, buddy." Shepherd ripped off the wrapper and stuffed the gum into his mouth. While he chewed, he took the ring and carefully placed it back in the little blue velvet box and then tucked the box up under the visor. He turned to us. "Well, *mi amigos,* what do you think? Is she going to say yes?"

Gus shrugged. "Who?" he asked. He was staring at Shepherd's mouth and I could tell that now he was wishing he hadn't given away the gum.

"Your mother." Shepherd blew a bubble and let it go flat. "The woman I love. The woman of my dreams. The woman I want to marry!"

I thought of the other person Shepherd was already married to, Sally. "Are you divorced yet?" I asked.

Shepherd wrinkled his forehead. "That's a valid question, Annie. And technically, no," he admitted. "But I'm just waiting on the paperwork at this point."

"Yes," Gus said, still staring at Shepherd's gum-chewing. "She would say yes."

"Maybe," I said, kicking my heels on the top of the toolbox. "She would probably say maybe."

"Maybe's good enough for me," Shepherd told us, smiling. "That's at least getting my foot in the door. So what do you think of this view?" He chewed his bubble gum hard and flung his hand out to point at the barn, the field, the water far in the distance. "This is the spot I've picked out to pop the question." He stopped. "You wouldn't have to call me Dad. But I'd like you to consider it."

"It's pretty here," I said. I reached down and picked up my book off the floor of the truck and pretended to read the back cover. It had a photograph of the girl giving one of her horses a kiss on the nose. "Mom had to go away for a while," I told Shepherd, not looking at him. "But she's back now."

"I'd like a chocolate chip ice cream cone," Gus said, tapping Shepherd's knee. "Or a piece of gum."

"I know your mother's had some tough times, believe me," Shepherd said. He grabbed Gus's hand where it was tapping. Then he took mine and squeezed them both the way you squeeze an almost empty tube of toothpaste or something you are trying to crush. "I know about her going away. I know all about it. But that's what I'm here to tell you two. My love has never been stronger. I'm a man in love. A man on fire! No fooling! I would not lie."

"You should probably tell her yourself," I said, pulling my hand away from his.

"Oh lord, I would," Shepherd sighed, turning the key to start the truck. "But she keeps on hanging up every last damn time she hears my voice." He smiled. "Your mother likes me a lot. I just don't think she knows it."

When he dropped us off exactly where he'd picked us up

on State Street, a few minutes later, Shepherd put one finger to his lips. "You really don't have to mention this," he said, leaning out the rolled-down window. "I've got a plan but it requires us to work in secret, as a united front, as a team. Can I have a show of support? Who would like to be on my team?"

Gus raised his arm. I folded mine across my chest and stared up at a blackbird bobbing on an electric line.

"Good enough," Shepherd told us. "One and a half. I can work with that."

At home our mother was crouched on the floor in the living room, painting one of the wooden chairs from the kitchen bright yellow. She had newspapers spread out all over the Oriental rug to catch the drips and her hair was done up on top of her head in some kind of fancy bun like a mermaid or a ballerina might wear.

"I was starting to worry," she told us, looking at her watch.

There were yellow streaks circling her arms. Ever since she had gotten back from Silverlawns, a few days before, she had been redecorating our whole house, mostly painting the furniture and walls all different bright colors.

"I guess we were walking pretty slow," I told her. I hung my jacket in the hall closet and went and sat on the edge of the couch. Outside the big picture window, the shadows from the tall trees in the yard were deep and black. In two days it would be Halloween, and every night it was getting dark earlier and earlier.

"What did you learn today?" my mother asked Gus. She stood and kissed him on the forehead and left a yellow smear near his eyebrow. I watched the brush she was holding drip on the corner of the coffee table she had painted cherry red on Tuesday.

"We practiced cursive writing the letter R and the number seven," Gus told her. "But I was bored so Miss Hill let me write a story instead." He pulled a folded piece of wide-lined paper from his pocket and handed it to our mother. "It's about a family of Martians and their pet raccoon who has rabies."

"That's great, sweetheart." My mother set the paper on the fireplace mantel and rubbed her hand on Gus's head. When she pulled it away, his hair stuck up in small yellow clumps. "I'll read it in a while. I just need to finish with this chair."

"What's for dinner?" I asked my mother. Now she was kneeling and peering at something under the television. When no one answered, I reached up and grabbed Gus's story and started reading it out loud. *The Marshans were not happy with thare new pet,* it began. "This is all wrong," I told Gus.

"Give it!" he screamed. I held the paper too high for him to jump, but after he'd tried to bite me hard on the knee, my mother put down her paintbrush and turned to us. "There is a chicken in the oven," she said. "Please stop that."

"I would like to tell you what other interesting thing I did today," Gus said. He had his Martian story and was folding it into a square.

"No, you wouldn't." I put my hand over his mouth, just for a second.

"I can see that I'm not going to get to finish painting this chair." My mother sighed and adjusted her bun, which had sagged to one side. "Why don't you go and wash your hands and faces and I'll make a salad." She stared at the couch. "How much do you hate that pattern?" she asked us.

"A lot," Gus said. "So much."

"Me, too." My mother frowned and bit her lip.

The couch, the same one we had always had, was covered in a fabric of big roses and twisting leaves and vines. "This is going to be a tough one." My mother ran her hand over one of the smooth, flowery couch cushions. "Hopeless," she said.

"I like it," I told her. "Please don't paint it."

My mother laughed, but I saw that her eyes had shifted up and were already watching something out the window, a bird moving in the shadowy branches, a star showing suddenly in the dark blue sky. Her lips barely moved when she smiled. "That's funny," she said. "That's not a bad idea."

Later, we ate dinner standing up because all the chairs around the kitchen table were still too sticky to sit on. Gus and I made circles of thumbprints in the soft paint on their seats while we waited for our mother to pour two glasses of milk. When she was closing the spout on the cardboard carton, I tried to picture Shepherd's ring on one of her thin fingers.

"This is just like a picnic," she told us, leaning on the splotchy, bright green dish cabinet and passing out napkins. "Except there aren't any ants."

"And we're in our own kitchen." I held my plate in one

hand and swallowed a forkful of rice. I had my back against the humming refrigerator.

"And we can't sit down," Gus added.

I took a sip of milk. "And there's no lemonade and no watermelon or brownies."

"And for instance, on a picnic you can lie on the dirt and grass if you feel like it." Gus stood on his tiptoes and laid his head on the counter to demonstrate. "I would probably look like this," he said.

"And also . . . ," I started.

"Okay, okay, all right, I get it," our mother mumbled, poking at a piece of tomato.

She chewed, thinking. Her long hair was loose around her shoulders now, and one strand hung curled over her cheek like a line drawn there by accident. Since she had been back I had been noticing the new things about her, how she moved more carefully or the way she held her face absolutely still when she thought no one was looking, the little bits of her that were not the same as before. I wondered all the time what had happened at Silverlawns, but when I tried to picture anything, with my eyes shut tight, I could only see my mother alone, walking across grass the color of old nickels, a kind of dream. That was all. I tried not to ask her too much about what it had been like because when I did she would only say, "Nothing, really. Nothing important." Now I watched her taking small bites of everything, the three of us standing there in the bright kitchen.

"I know this isn't a picnic," she told us after a minute. "But would it actually hurt you to use your imaginations?"

We ate quietly, listening to the tree branches brushing the windows in the wind outside. No one said anything until Gus took a big slug of milk and put his plate in the sink. He hadn't touched his chicken leg.

"Would you like to get married?" he asked.

"Where in the world did you get that idea?" My mother coughed and put her napkin up to her lips.

"I was just wondering," Gus said, moving his foot when I tried to kick it. "If you thought you might."

"That's sweet of you to wonder," my mother told him. "But it's a moot point on a number of levels."

"Moot," Gus repeated.

"It means I'm not getting married anytime soon." She turned and started running water over the dishes. I saw her push Gus's chicken leg into the disposal. "No cookies for you," she told him.

"But if someone did ask," Gus went on, hopping to miss me again, "you would say yes."

"Ha!" my mother said. "I would say ha."

"Really?" Gus frowned and I tried to pinch him on the arm to get him to shut up.

"Well, maybe not *ha* exactly," our mother decided, wiping her hands on a paper towel. "But some variation on that. Right now, I'm concentrating on getting my act together." She looked around the kitchen, at the blue-and-white-striped wallpaper that was half peeled off along one whole corner. "Plus, I'm redecorating the house."

"Hmmm," Gus said. He was on the floor, pulling a bag of Oreos from the bottom cupboard.

"Does that answer your question?" my mother asked. She had gone over to the doorway and was tugging at a piece of the ripped wallpaper.

"No." Gus showed his teeth. They were black with crushed Oreo. "No, it doesn't."

"Yes, it does," I told him. "It really does."

The phone rang late at night. It was true that I might have been asleep. "Oh, it's you," I thought I could hear my mother saying to someone in the dark. "It's just you." Then there was muttering, things I couldn't quite understand. I pulled my quilt up around my ears and I didn't dream exactly, but instead I kept picturing Shepherd's scarred hand opening a blue box. Inside were tiny stars in a small sky, a whole tiny world. "You'd be surprised," his voice kept repeating. "I bet you'd be surprised." It seemed more real than something that had actually happened in real life.

In the morning when our mother drove us to school I was still thinking about the dream. I was expecting something to happen. That's when I caught a glimpse of Shepherd's truck parked on a side street, next to the barbershop.

"He's probably getting a haircut," Gus said, spotting the truck, too. Gus was sitting in the front seat, eating the banana our mother had put in his lunch box.

"He who?" my mother asked. She was wearing a white shirt with paint smears all over the front and a pair of old jeans.

Earlier, she had dropped the coffeepot on the kitchen floor, making a pond of coffee and broken glass near the stove, and now she was not paying attention to stop signs.

"Are you going to pick us up this afternoon?" I leaned into the front seat and rested my chin on her shoulder. I could see the speedometer. "We're going fifty-seven in a thirty-five zone," I told her. "In case you weren't noticing."

"Who's probably getting a haircut?" she asked, stepping on the brake, but only a little. She flicked on the turn signal. "Who are you talking about?" By then we were in front of the school, stopped by the double glass doors. I saw Mrs. Birdsall, my teacher, carrying a big bag across the parking lot. Even from far away I could see that she looked tired, and that meant that we would spend the first two hours of class reading silently to ourselves out of our science books until it was time for recess.

"I'll see you at three fifteen, Paige," Gus told our mother. He held his banana peel in one hand and patted her with the other.

"I'm Mom to you, young man, remember?" Our mother gave him a disappointed frown. "We've discussed this before. Extensively."

Two second graders, Heidi Kistler and Sarah Kigoma, walked in front of our car and stared. When I turned away from them, I saw that Shepherd had parked his truck in the teachers' parking lot, over near the flagpole. He waved both his arms in circles the way people do in movies when they're lost on a desert island and they want the plane to rescue them. I waved back once and then tried not to look at him.

"Mom," Gus was saying. "I have a tooth that's about to fall out." He pointed into his mouth. "It's moving around quite a bit."

"Okay, okay, you're fine," she mumbled, putting on her sunglasses. "And I'd like you to walk home again today. You children need some fresh air and exercise."

"We do?" I asked. She had never mentioned exercise before.

"Yes," she said. "It's part of our new plan."

"What plan?" I thought it probably had to do with her redecorating the house.

"Our plan," she said, sighing. "The new one."

While I gathered my books and shut the car door, I peered out of the corner of my eye. I could see that Shepherd had quit circling his arms.

"His hair is pretty short," Gus said, coming to stand beside me. "I liked it better when it was all over his head. And now he doesn't have a beard, either." We watched Shepherd while our mother squealed out of the school driveway and floored it onto State Street. Shepherd gave us the thumbs-up when she had disappeared past some maple trees.

"Just checking in!" he shouted to us across the parking lot. "Keep up the great teamwork, amigos!" He got into his truck and pulled away fast, following in the direction our mother had gone. The three fifth graders on safety patrol had turned to watch him.

"What's he talking about?" Gus asked.

I shook my head. Gus had dropped his banana peel on the sidewalk. "Someone could slip on that," I told him. "Don't litter."

"Most of the time, I don't understand what Shepherd is

saying," Gus admitted. He set one foot on the banana peel and pretended to fall backward. "I guess when he and Mom get married, we'll all go and live in his apartment. Then we'll probably talk more and he can explain what he means."

"I doubt it," I said, moving toward the glass doors, which were decorated with construction paper cutouts of witches and pumpkins. The first bell had rung and other kids were pushing in around us.

"That's too bad," Gus said. "I've really liked him for quite a while."

"You're not the one who has to marry him," I told Gus. I saw that he had picked up the banana peel and was carrying it clutched in one hand. Now we were inside, under the bright fluorescent lights that made Gus look even smaller and paler than he already was.

"Oh, I know that," he said. "Mom has to marry him."

All the way home that afternoon, Gus and I kept our eyes open for Shepherd's truck, but it was nowhere. When we turned on our street and got close to our house, I could see that Aunt Claire's car was parked in the driveway.

"Uh-oh," I said.

"What?" Gus asked.

"Nothing," I told him. "Just don't say a thing."

Gus and I dropped our jackets and books in the front hall and went to the dining room, where our mother was showing Aunt Claire the purple trim she had just finished over the doorway. When she saw us, she smiled and winked.

"Children." Aunt Claire bent to kiss us on both cheeks. She was wearing a beige raincoat and she hadn't put down her purse.

"Then I thought I'd do this in something pink or maybe off-blue." My mother pointed to the ceiling. "Something to lighten and lift."

The four of us stared up at the light fixture, at the streak the color of flamingos that our mother had already put near it.

"Will you two excuse us for a moment?" Aunt Claire asked. She patted our backs and one of her rings was hard on my shoulder. "Why don't you go and get a snack and then I want to hear all about what you've been up to this week."

Gus and I went and stood in the kitchen and ate handfuls of raisins from a box on the counter. The yellow chairs were lined up on both sides of the table, glistening in the late afternoon sun. A bouquet of flowers in a vase tied with a ribbon sat in the middle of it all, next to the sugar bowl. Without even trying, I could hear Aunt Claire and my mother talking.

"I don't like the looks of this," Aunt Claire was saying.

"It's not your house," my mother snapped. "I've never particularly liked your taste, either."

For a minute, it was quiet. "Here, have an Oreo," Gus whispered, pressing one into my hand. While I chewed, I wandered over to the table and read the little card that was lying beside the vase of flowers. *"Roses for a rose,"* it said. Then underneath in smaller letters: *"These are daisies, but I hope, God willing, you know what I mean. Love, Shepherd."* I folded the card and put it in my pocket.

"Are you taking your medication?" Aunt Claire's voice

asked. "Honestly, Paige, do you have any idea how much I've paid for your treatment? I might have a new car instead."

"Oh, please." My mother sighed. "Don't make a federal case out of this, okay, Claire? I'm just redecorating a little. I would like a kind of new start. A clean slate. If that's all right with you."

"Purple," Aunt Claire said. "Explain that."

I imagined the way Aunt Claire was standing then, holding her purse close to her side, keeping her chin high and her neck stiff while she stared up at the pink-streaked ceiling, at the color around the window frames. For a second, I felt sorry for her. Then I felt sorry for Shepherd. I could hear something being dragged over the floor, maybe the stepladder.

Gus tugged at my sleeve. "Today in school my tooth fell out during story circle." He showed me a tiny white stub. "It's worth a dollar. Or more."

"That's great," I whispered. "Be quiet."

"Well, of course it's up to you," Aunt Claire said, finally. "But I'm watching this whole situation. Tell the children I'll talk to them tomorrow."

"There's no situation," my mother said. "Really." She coughed. The front door creaked open and someone's heels clicked in quick steps.

"Oh, there's a situation here," Aunt Claire's voice said then. "There most certainly is a situation."

That night after dinner, Gus and I sat in our jackets on the front steps carving faces into the pumpkins our mother had gotten at the grocery store. I could see my breath under the porch light, and the wind in the dark trees in the yard was making the sound of a car driving away, slow and faint. Inside, past the half-closed curtains, our mother was standing on the stepladder, talking on the phone and pushing a paintbrush over the ceiling.

Earlier, all during dinner, I had wanted to ask her about the bouquet of flowers, about Shepherd, but whenever I had started to say something, I had stopped.

"What is it?" she'd asked me finally, placing her fork along the edge of her plate. The three of us were in the shiny yellow chairs, my mother and I facing each other across the bouquet. Behind my mother's head the striped wallpaper hung in skinny, torn strips from the back wall. She'd rested her chin in her hands and smiled at me in her faraway way. "Sometimes I look at you and I just think. I think . . ." She didn't finish but made a swirl with her hand in the air.

"I like these," I'd said, pointing at one of the daisies when it had been quiet for too long.

"Me, too," Gus had added.

"Oh, those." My mother had gotten up by then and was clearing the dishes. "They're all right, I suppose."

Now, sitting on the porch, I could feel the sharp paper corner of Shepherd's card cutting into my leg through my pocket. I leaned back against the wooden chest of drawers my mother had dragged from her bedroom earlier, and I dug at the inside of my jack-o'-lantern with a spoon, pulling out orange seeds and strings.

"It shouldn't have three eyes," I told Gus when he turned his pumpkin so I could see it.

"I was trying to make it look like a Martian." He worked on the pumpkin's mouth with a dull knife. "There's a situation here," he said.

"Don't repeat things you don't even understand," I told him. "You do that all the time." I grabbed a handful of the slippery seeds and tossed one in his direction.

"I know what 'situation' means." He sat his pumpkin on the porch railing. In addition to three eyes, it also had pointy teeth and a square nose. "A situation is what we have. There's one here."

Our mother opened the front door and stood in her socks on the bristly mat. "Beautiful," she said when we showed her our pumpkins. She took a picture with the camera she was holding.

"Smile," she said after it had flashed. "Just lovely."

"You mean scary." Gus frowned and cradled his jack-o'-lantern.

"Didn't I say scary?" our mother asked. "I meant to say scary."

As she bent to put the candles inside of first Gus's pumpkin, then mine, her hair hung in a long wave along one side of her neck and over her shoulder. It was cold and the wind was loud now, the stars showing once and then disappearing under the purple-black clouds. I shivered and held my arms. Our mother was humming something as she moved to turn off the porch light.

"Here," she said, and when she struck the match and lowered it to the candles her shadowed smile went golden for half a second. There was only the bright circle of her face, eyes shut in the dark, the way someone looks when they are wishing above a birthday cake, just before it all goes out. She blew on the match.

We stood and stared at the glowing pumpkins on the railing. They seemed to be floating, and for a few minutes no one said anything. When Gus sneezed, our mother clapped her hands and turned on the porch light. The three of us blinked at one another. "Okay, go and get cleaned up and we'll figure out what you're going to be tomorrow," my mother said.

"A pirate," Gus said. "I already told you that."

"Of course you did." My mother squatted to pick up the spoons and the newspapers covered with pumpkin seeds. "A pirate. Now I remember. And Annie?" she asked.

"I'm not sure," I said. I watched my jack-o'-lantern flickering. "I could be anything this year, I guess."

"Well, I think I know." My mother tapped her chin with one of the spoons. "I can absolutely picture you. Okay, let's get going."

Upstairs Gus and I ran hot water and washed the sticky pumpkin off our hands. Gus rubbed with the white towel hanging on the hook behind the door, and I stared in the mirror. I poked at a freckle and traced a strand of my hair, which was no color there was a word for exactly, except maybe hay or dry wheat, something left in a field at the end of summer. I wondered if even once I would ever look like my mother had, her face glowing and beautiful in the dark.

"Ha, I see you," Gus said, grinning. "You probably think you're pretty."

"I know you're not," I told him, grabbing the towel and pulling it over his head. "And no one asked you, anyway."

While Gus and I were yanking at the towel, the phone rang and I could hear my mother answering it in the hall at the bottom of the stairs. I crept to the banister. "Yes, I told you I got them, thank you," she was saying. There was a long silence. "No, I can't take a drive with you right now. Of course not."

My mother cleared her throat. "That would be a very bad idea," she said, sighing. "Very, very bad."

When Gus and I came downstairs, our mother had changed her mind about our Halloween costumes. "I hadn't realized how late it was," she told us. She glanced at the ceiling, which was hot pink over one whole corner and light blue in a small blotch near the window. "Truthfully, I'm not crazy about either of these," she told us, pointing up. "Okay, how about this: I'll work on your costumes tonight, and in the morning, they'll be all ready for you."

"No, Paige." Gus stamped one foot.

"Ahem," my mother said. "Excuse me?"

"No," Gus said. "Mom. I need a black cover for my eye and a parrot on my shoulder."

"I think I can handle that." My mother smiled at him and walked us back upstairs. The rug from the hall was now at the door to my bedroom. Two paintings from the living room were hanging near the light switch.

"Also, I have a tooth that I'm putting under my pillow." Gus showed her the stub. "I almost forgot."

"Okay," my mother said. "Thanks for letting me know. I'll tell the tooth fairy."

While Gus went to get into his pajamas, my mother rearranged the sweaters on the shelf in my closet. She was trying to put everything into three neat stacks. I sat on the edge of my quilt and took Shepherd's card out of my pocket. I unfolded it and saw the word *roses*. I looked over at the window, at the new curtains so pale the moon shone right through them.

"Someone is probably in love with you," I told my mother.

Her back went still. She stopped straightening a green sweater.

"He thinks he is," she said softly, without turning around. "There's a big difference." She came and sat on the bed next to me and took my hand. I was still holding the card. Her forehead crinkled as she studied my face. "You shouldn't be concerning yourself with any of this," she told me. "It's not for you to think about. I hope you're not."

"I'm not," I said. "But I was still wondering if you might be in love with him a little bit."

My mother looked away for a second. When she turned back to me her face was smooth and unworried, the way it was in all the black-and-white photographs I had seen stuffed in the bottom drawer of the living room cabinet: Aunt Claire and my mother on horses; my mother in a shiny dress standing in front of a Christmas tree; my mother and a smiling boy pinning her with a flower—the pictures of the times before. Then she pressed her fingers to her forehead and the look was gone.

"I was wondering," I told her.

"Annie, Annie," she said and hugged me close. The collar of her shirt smelled like turpentine, like gasoline. I imagined I could feel the bones in her entire body. She let me go and pushed my hair behind my ears. "I can't be in love right now."

"You might be," I said. "You could like him and not even know it."

She shook her head. "Shhh." She walked over and shut the closet doors. "I love you," she said. "And I want you to go to sleep."

In the morning a pair of cardboard wings was tied to my bedpost. One wing was a little bigger than the other, cut jagged on the corners, and both were covered in lace paper doilies and edged in long ribbons. I stared at them for a while from my pillow, and then I got up and tried them on over my nightgown, tying the loops of ribbons once around my neck, and the others in a bow tight across my chest. In the scratchy mirror over my dresser the wings didn't look real exactly, but more like two pieces of curving cardboard sticking out from my back. They knocked against each other when I moved. Gus was running up and down the hall in a black felt eye patch and striped pants. He was yelling and waving a dollar bill.

"You don't have to wear them if you don't like them." My mother stood in the doorway, holding a blue paintbrush.

"No, they're great," I told her.

"Are you sure? You won't hurt my feelings if they're not what you want."

"I want them," I said. They weren't at all what I might have chosen.

"Good." She smiled, leaning in the blue door frame, and I watched the paintbrush drip once, in slow motion, onto her bare foot. "I'm so glad."

* * *

In school that day I had to sit bent forward because the stiff wings kept hitting my chair. My white leotard was too tight in the arms. Other kids who were dressed as tubes of toothpaste or dice or boxes of cereal couldn't sit down at all. Mrs. Birdsall had on a witch's hat and her regular clothes. She read to us for a while from a story about real-life haunted houses and then made us go through our math homework, problem by problem. No one seemed very excited about Halloween, except the younger kids, who we could hear screaming from their classrooms down the hall.

"What are you, anyway?" Andy Keeler leaned over my desk and asked before geography hour. He was wearing a raincoat like that guy from the detective show on TV.

"Sort of an angel," I told him. I pulled at a small tear where a hole was starting in the knee of my white tights.

"It's really hard to tell that," he said, looking me over. "I thought you were probably some kind of a bird."

"I thought that, too," Jennifer Peshawbi said, turning in her desk. "You should just say you're a bird. It would be a lot easier."

I shrugged and my wings made a scraping sound, like ripping paper, against the back of my chair.

At three Gus and I walked home along State Street. It was warm enough so that we didn't have to wear our jackets. I helped him carry his plastic jack-o'-lantern, which was already half full and heavy with candy. He had just eaten three Tootsie Pops in a row. "It's okay because I plan to get much more later," he was explaining. His black eye patch was pushed up on his forehead and he kept skipping ahead of me. When we turned a corner, I could see that Shepherd had pulled his truck over down at the end of the block and was waiting for us, leaning against the front bumper.

"You look great!" he yelled when we were still a few houses away. "An angel and a pirate! Wow, I wish I had my camera."

"You can tell I'm supposed to be an angel?" I asked when we got up next to him.

"Sure. What else would you be?" He handed us each a Snickers bar. "Listen, I need to call a team meeting. I think tonight's the night. Why don't I give you a ride home and we can talk."

I untied my angel wings and held them with my jacket as Shepherd helped us up. After we'd gotten into the truck, Shepherd started it and then put his head on the steering wheel for a second. He had his palm flat over the pocket of his shirt where his name was embroidered. It looked like he wasn't even breathing. A lady who was sweeping her front walk near where we were parked had stopped and was staring at us, craning her neck to see inside the truck.

"Are you okay?" Gus asked. He had already ripped open his candy bar and was taking big bites.

"I'm overwhelmed," Shepherd said, not moving his head. Then he sat up and put the truck in gear. "Well, that's passed. Sometimes I just feel the full weight of my love for your mother and I can't move."

Gus rubbed at a piece of caramel that was stuck to his pirate vest. "That never happens to me," he said.

We ate our candy bars and drove in silence up to the field where Shepherd had first shown us the ring. We parked on the hill and looked out past the roof of the barn at the flat, endless lake. The weeds that had been golden before were already turning brown.

"My divorce came through yesterday," Shepherd told us. He reached over and pulled the little blue velvet box from the glove compartment. "I'm ready to make my move."

"Have you talked to her?" I asked. I stared at Shepherd's scarred hand clenching the blue box. It was shaking.

"That's my plan," Shepherd said, still staring off in the distance. "I'm going to talk to her tonight. Ask her, I mean. You might have noticed that I got a haircut and generally tried to clean myself up a bit to get ready." He ran his fingers over his head and put one finger on his cheek. "It just occurs to me. This won't be much of a view in the dark."

"You won't be able to see anything in the dark," Gus said.

The three of us stared at the far, silvery water.

"Some things are so obvious that you don't even think of them," Shepherd decided. He put the velvet box back in the glove compartment. He hadn't even shown us the ring again.

"I'll come up with something else, I guess. A slightly different strategy." He turned toward Gus and me. "Well, this is it, compadres," he said. "Any final advice?"

I shook my head and concentrated on Shepherd's name patch, the embroidered circle over his heart. I knew it didn't matter that my mother didn't love Shepherd. I couldn't think of one thing that would stop him.

Gus was poking around inside his plastic pumpkin for more candy. "Our mother's redecorating the house. She's painting the ceiling pink," he told Shepherd.

"That woman." Shepherd smiled. "She's full of surprises." He let out a deep breath and started the truck.

"I can't thank you enough for your help with all of this," Shepherd said, as we drove back down through the field and out the open gate. "I couldn't have done it without you."

"We didn't do anything," I told him. I watched the trees and fences go flickering past like a too-fast movie.

"We did a lot," Gus said.

"And I won't forget it," Shepherd added. He turned on our street and stopped a few houses away from our own. All our neighbors were gone for the season, their windows shuttered and still. No one was watching when Shepherd got out and came around to open the passenger door. After he'd helped us down, Gus handed him a bubble-gum cigar.

"You are the two best friends a guy could have," Shepherd said, turning the green cigar over and over. He opened and closed his mouth. "Sometime, when things are different, we're going to . . ." He put the cigar in his pocket. "Wish me luck, okay?"

"Good luck," Gus said.

We watched Shepherd drive away. "Do you understand what's going on?" I asked Gus when the truck had disappeared. I had my cardboard wings tucked under my arm. "Do you know what Shepherd's talking about?"

"Yes." He nodded. "No."

At home, our mother was sitting at the dining room table, drinking a cup of tea. All the cans of paint were gone and most of the furniture was back where it should have been. "You just missed your aunt Claire," our mother told us, kissing Gus on the cheek. "Did you have fun at school?"

"I ate three Tootsie Pops and a Snickers bar," Gus said, "but I had more fun after school."

"What did Aunt Claire want?" I asked. I looked up at the ceiling, which was now completely light blue with swirls of white for the clouds. Being underneath it was exactly like standing outside on a nice day.

"Aunt Claire wanted to bother me," my mother said. She crinkled her forehead and took a sip of tea. "Oh, I didn't mean that the way it sounded," she added. "But Claire does bother me sometimes." She scratched at an invisible mark on the table. "Some people just don't get it."

"Get what?" I asked, but by then my mother was already walking toward the kitchen. "Don't eat any more candy," she called to Gus. "I mean it. You're going to make yourself ill."

Gus was lying on his back on the Oriental rug, holding his stomach. He had put his black felt eye patch back over one eye. "See," he said, smiling and pointing at the ceiling. "It's like the sky."

That night, as soon as it was dark, Gus and I went trick-or-treating. I had wanted to stay at home to see what Shepherd was going to do, but I knew that Gus couldn't be out by himself. I also knew that it was probably better if no one else was there when Shepherd took the small velvet box out of his glove compartment and tried to give it to our mother.

It had gotten cold and I had my angel wings tied over my winter jacket. For two hours, I followed Gus from door to door, as we filled our grocery sacks with Red Hots and M&M's and candy corn, but I couldn't care about any of it. I kept picturing Shepherd, his scarred hands holding out the misshapen ring. Gus walked ahead of me, counting everything we'd gotten. After an old man gave us pencils and then made us stand on his porch while he told us all about Jesus and God and how we'd better hurry up and find God fast, I told Gus that I thought it was time to quit.

"If the next house gives us an apple or a penny, we're going home," I said.

"It's okay." Gus adjusted his eye patch under a streetlight. His breath came out in silver puffs. "I'm ready to go now, anyway."

We started toward home, and a group of ghosts and devils pushed past us, running in the other direction. "That one was Charlie Swiss," Gus said. "He tried to hit me once."

"Yeah," I told him. "I remember."

We passed some other trick-or-treaters, one policeman, one Batman, two cats, some older kids who weren't even wearing costumes. We didn't talk until we were on our street, which was dark and empty.

"I had fun," Gus told me. "I didn't have a great time, but it was all right."

"Okay," I said. "Good."

He grabbed my elbow and we made our way over the bumpy sidewalk. My wings flapped and snapped against each other with every step. Gus started talking about what he was going to do with all of his candy. Somewhere someone was having a bonfire and I could smell burning leaves and ashes blowing through the dark. Up ahead, I saw Shepherd's truck parked in our driveway. As we got closer, I could see that every light was turned on inside our house, all the windows yellow and throwing their brightness out on the lawn.

We came up the walk and stood with our sacks of candy on the front steps. Gus had stopped chewing his licorice whip. Now I could smell smoke. "Do you . . . ?" Gus started to ask. I shook my head.

Inside, we called for our mother, but no one answered. I didn't want to move. The walls were shiny in their new colors and everything ordinary—the glass vase on the side table, an oval mirror I'd seen a million times before—was different and almost alive in all of that light. I untied my wings and left them on the red cabinet. "Hello, hello!" Gus kept yelling as we wandered down the hall.

In the living room I noticed the empty space where the couch usually sat. In the kitchen there were two glasses on the counter, ice melting in the clear bottoms of each. I touched the cool side of one with my finger. Gus and I cupped our hands and peered out the window at the big backyard, where something was on fire, there in the blackness, where the grass sloped down to the lake. The flames were high and orange and perfectly in one place, like the pictures you see of a cowboy campfire in the desert or a pirate ship burning on the ocean; one thing on fire and nothing else in the world.

We went outside, letting the door close behind us. We stood and watched. Music was playing on a radio set up on the back porch. It was a slow song with a man's sad voice and a guitar. I had heard it before. I almost knew the words. Shepherd and my mother were holding each other and dancing on the grass, in the glow of the burning couch.

In the morning the couch, or what was left of it, was gone. Shepherd had taken it away in his truck when he left at midnight. In the early sun I went and walked in my nightgown and bare feet on the frosted lawn and saw the singed circle where it had been. At breakfast, when my mother told us that she had always hated the couch, that it was old and ugly, that it was the easiest way to get rid of it, it might have made sense. I knew you could love someone and believe them. You sometimes could.

"I didn't know you could do that," Gus had said, pointing out the window with his cereal spoon to the burned place in the yard where the couch had been. I had known what he meant.

My mother had looked at him over her teacup.

"You can't," I'd told him, before she could speak. "You really can't."

But that was after. That night Shepherd and my mother hadn't seen us yet. He had his hand on her back and they were twirling and spinning in the dark.

HERE WE ARE

We liked things best after they were gone, and even better if we'd never had them at all.

"Is that true?" I asked my mother, since she was the one who had just said it. We were fighting about getting a dog and that was her reason.

She thought for a second. "Yes, I believe so. For instance, when I was growing up we had a very mean dachshund named Sammy. I never liked Sammy, not one bit, not until the day he ran away. Then . . ." She paused. "I missed him like crazy. I loved that dog! It would have been better if we'd never had him to begin with. Now I can't look at a dog and not think of poor Sammy."

"That's a terrible story," I said.

"Oh, you're right." I could hear her let out a long breath. "Please forget that I ever came up with that one."

It was late November and it still hadn't snowed. The three of us were lying on our backs in the yard on the tough brown grass, watching a jet leave a perfectly straight line across the sky. We were waiting for Shepherd Nash, the man who was in love with our mother, to deliver a piano she didn't want him to give to her. We were waiting outside because my mother wanted us to get fresh air, and also because she liked to slow Shepherd down as much as possible. "And that means catching him while he's still in the driveway" was how she had put it.

We had been in the yard for ten minutes. Gus was beside me, sweeping his arms and legs flat on the ground like one of those wooden puppets with the string that you pull to make them jump. I listened to his jacket crinkling and uncrinkling, his boots scraping half moons in the frozen dirt. "If you're making fake snow angels," I told him, "quit it."

My mother tried again. "Here's a better example: Right now, you wish that it was winter, a real winter. But if there were three feet of snow, you probably wouldn't be very happy about it."

We were all sitting up now, staring past the side of the house at the big lake, which was as smooth and dark as the back of a mirror. "I'd be happy." Gus nodded. Pieces of dry grass were stuck to his head.

"People who have never experienced winter, on the other hand," our mother went on, "think it would be absolutely wonderful. They can imagine the good things about it." She leaned over and brushed the grass from Gus's hair. "People in Brazil dream about snow."

"I know." Gus nodded again.

"I don't think so," I said. I bit at the tip of my mitten. The red wool was gritty against my teeth. Three weeks before, our mother had taken a part-time job in the bookstore downtown. The store was never very busy, so most of the time our mother looked at books. Every day she told us one amazing thing she had read. I didn't believe most of the things. "Not all people in Brazil dream about snow," I told her.

"Oh, it's true." My mother stood and slapped at her jeans. "I was just reading about it."

"I had a dream that we got a dog," Gus said.

"All right, all right." My mother buttoned the top button of her coat and stamped her feet in the cold. "I get the picture."

"You're about to have something you don't want," I told my mother.

"I'm making the best of a bad situation," she said. "That's different from going out and buying a dog. But I see your point."

We watched Shepherd's truck coming down the street. It sounded like a loud train and the whole thing leaned to the left. A squirrel darted out from our neighbors', the Slocums', cedar hedge and ran between the tires. You could see Shepherd inside, jerking the steering wheel hard to miss it.

"He's driving much too fast. Not to mention that he's transporting a piano, for God's sake," my mother said.

"You usually drive a lot faster than that," I pointed out.

"Not when I have a piano, I don't." My mother was silent as Shepherd squealed into the driveway and stopped. Gus and I took a step backward. Shepherd smiled and pointed with his thumb to a huge shape tied in the back of the truck. "Not if I had a piano, I wouldn't," my mother mumbled.

"Here I am," Shepherd said, getting out and opening the tailgate latch flat. He was wearing a jacket that said NASH ELEC-TRIC over his heart. "Sorry I'm late."

He bent to kiss our mother on the cheek, but she turned

and he kissed her ear instead. Shepherd shrugged. "Okay," he said, clapping his hands. "Harvey Kewaygo is going to be here in a minute to help me get this into the house." He patted the shape, covered in a green bedspread and wrapped with rope. "Would anyone like a sneak preview?"

"Yes!" Gus yelled.

"Shepherd," my mother said, "I know you don't believe me, but as I told you, I really don't want a piano. It's very sweet of you, but I really can't play and—"

Shepherd held up his hands. "Too late." He laughed. "Watch this." He cut the rope with his jackknife and in one pull, the way I'd seen a magician on TV yank a tablecloth from underneath a complete dinner, Shepherd threw off the bedspread and showed us his gift. "He's a little unusual looking, I realize." Shepherd ran his fingers over the top of the piano. "But get to know him."

"Him," Gus repeated.

"I like to think of the piano as a masculine instrument." Shepherd coughed.

The piano was a dull brown and had scars and gashes up and down all sides, as if someone had gone after it with something sharp. The initials J.H. were carved inside a heart near the keyboard. There was a little painting of a moose in the upper left corner. My mother was staring at it with her mouth open. I moved closer to get a better look, and when I stood on my tiptoes and ran my fingers over the dark wood, I could feel hundreds of tiny grooves and marks. When I squinted I could see that the marks were people's phone numbers, written in hard ballpoint pen or cut with safety pins.

"This is just . . ." my mother began, but didn't finish.

"I know what you mean! Amazing, right?" Shepherd said.

He squatted on a cardboard box in the back of the truck and began to play, dancing his hands over the white keys. The music came out in plinks and plunks, muffled then loud, muffled then loud again, like a fair sounds when you're walking toward it from a block away. Shepherd sang: "I dedicate this to Paige, Annie, and Gus, a little song about a man and his horse."

"Shepherd!" my mother called over the music, but he couldn't hear her. Instead, he played another song, one that Gus and I knew. We sang along for a verse when our mother turned away from us, getting a Kleenex out of her pocket to blow her nose.

"Join in!" Shepherd yelled. He was standing, banging on the piano, sending his music down the street and out over the flat gray lake. I imagined people a mile from our house hearing it, too. All of a sudden Shepherd stopped. "How selfish of me," he said. "This is your piano and here I am showing off, acting like he's mine."

Our mother shook her head. I wasn't sure if she was saying yes or no. "Now I know where I've seen this before," she said. "The Spot Bar, right?"

"Used to sit over by the pay phone next to the restroom," Shepherd smiled, hugging the side of the piano. "They were having a little sale, bar stools, shot glasses, and whatnot. New owner coming in. Thank God I got there in time to save him."

"Him," Gus said again.

"He means the piano," I told Gus. "He just explained that to you."

"This is what I was thinking." Shepherd spread his arms wide. "I was thinking that you, Paige, you could play a tambourine or something. I could play the piano. And the kids could sing harmony. Make it a regular family get-together, a little gathering. It'll be great!"

"Shepherd, may I speak with you for a second, please?" My mother was smiling, but she also looked scared. While she and Shepherd went over by the porch steps to talk, Gus and I climbed into the back of the truck to get a better look at the Spot Bar piano.

"769-4218," Gus read. "769-5013."

"For a time you won't forget or regret." I traced the words with one finger. "F-E-E-L," Gus spelled. "L-U-C-K-Y."

When Harvey Kewaygo pulled up in his van, Gus and I were reading a poem someone had carved near one of the foot pedals. Harvey waved to Shepherd and my mother, who were still arguing on the porch. Gus and I knew Harvey because he sometimes came to rake the leaves or mow the grass in Aunt Claire's yard. He was about seven feet tall and he always looked like he had just heard something that made him mad.

"Damn, that's ugly," he told us when we showed him the poem and some of the phone numbers. He scowled. "I wouldn't have that in my home."

"I know," I said. "But it's too late."

"I like it." Gus leaned against the piano. "Him."

"Well, let's get this show on the road," Harvey said. He peered under the piano. "Thank Jesus this thing's got wheels." He walked over to his van and started pulling out long boards and a metal cart with straps. By then, Shepherd and my mother had stopped talking. Gus and I went and stood with her on the lawn while Harvey and Shepherd pushed the piano down the ramp they had pieced together with the boards and shoved it out onto the driveway. They were both sweating even though it was freezing cold. Shepherd was humming, his breath coming out in a silver cloud. "Success!" he yelled, when they kept the piano from tipping into our mother's car.

When they stopped for a break, Harvey took off his flannel shirt and tied it around his head like a turban. Then he made a noise like an elephant or a bear charging, and the ugly piano went flying past us, up the sidewalk.

"This is such a good illustration of what we were discussing earlier," our mother whispered to Gus and me. "I used to love pianos, from afar. But now I may hate them forever."

"It's a nice gift," Gus said, adjusting his striped hat and taking our mother's gloved hand in his mittened one. "And you will love it. Like I will love my new dog. Which I will name Roger. Because he will be a him."

"Why do I even try?" my mother asked. We were watching Harvey and Shepherd leave huge tracks of splintered wood on the front porch steps as they pulled and leaned against the piano. They knocked over a wicker chair and a dead potted geranium. Everything shook. It went on for quite a while. My mother covered her eyes. When they finally got it upright on the porch and through the front door, Shepherd whooped and Harvey pounded him on the back.

"We're in business!" Shepherd called to us. He did a dance on the top step. "Come on in!"

"Another thing to consider is that we spend eighteen years

of our lives asleep," our mother said, after Shepherd and Harvey had disappeared inside our home, laughing and shouting. "I find some comfort in that fact at times like these."

Music was coming through the opened front door.

"I love him," Gus said, as we walked toward the house. "The piano."

I could tell that he really meant Shepherd.

That evening, our mother couldn't figure out where to put the piano, and for an hour she walked from room to room with her hands on her hips, frowning. Shepherd, who hadn't left yet, followed two feet behind her and said, "Here?" every few minutes. While they walked, Gus and I ate dinner with Harvey Kewaygo on TV trays our mother had set up for us in the living room. We were watching a show about alligators and their young.

"This is a comfortable couch," Harvey told us during a commercial. He had taken his flannel shirt off his head and now he was wearing it buttoned like a regular shirt. He was sitting up straight against the puffy cushions. He patted the couch and nodded while he chewed. "I believe it's down-filled," he said after he'd swallowed. "And of fairly high quality."

"It's a new couch," Gus said. "We had another one, but we had to get rid of it. My mom was redecorating."

Harvey pointed to the television. The alligators were in the water with only their eyes showing. When a white bird floated past, one of the alligators opened its jaws and the bird squawked once and disappeared. The other alligators slapped their tails, as if they were clapping. "That's why I'll never live in Florida," Harvey said.

After that, we ate for a while without talking. I snuck looks at Harvey as he cut his piece of pizza with his knife and fork and dabbed at the corners of his mouth with his napkin. Gus was sneaking looks at Harvey, too, and when he saw Harvey lay his knife flat across the edge of his plate and then take a bite with the fork held just so, he copied Harvey exactly, even turning his wrist a little to the left, the way Harvey had.

"Stop it," I whispered.

Harvey frowned at me.

"I was talking to Gus," I explained. "He has a problem."

Harvey stared at us. Then he turned back to the screen where the alligators were lying in the sun while one of the scientists hid in the bushes with a dart gun. "Nature is so cruel," Harvey sighed.

"How many children do you have?" Gus asked Harvey.

"None yet." Harvey pushed his empty plate to the far edge of his TV tray and crossed his arms. "But I'd like to have a big family one day. I'd like to have lots of kids."

"Do you have a wife?" Gus asked, and I tried to kick him in the ankle.

In the hall Shepherd was saying to my mother, "If you put it here, you can play while you're talking on the phone."

Harvey rubbed his forehead with one hand. "I have a girlfriend. We've been dating for about six months, but I don't think we're going to get married anytime soon. She's a little too wild for me. Plus, she's not the most reliable person, and that's an important quality, reliability, when you're considering someone for your life partner. Honesty is important. I also value a good sense of humor."

Gus nodded and pushed his plate across his TV tray, just the way Harvey had done.

We watched the rest of the alligator show and when the eight o'clock movie started, Harvey yawned and stretched his hands over his head. "This has been fun," he told us. "I appreciate you having me over for dinner." He got up and went and stood by the front door. He was so tall that he had to stoop in order to fit.

"Don't leave already!" Shepherd yelled as he and my mother came from the kitchen. "We're going to have a little family sing-along later. It's going to be great!"

"If Harvey has to leave, he has to leave," my mother said, smiling and touching Harvey's arm. It was almost like a small shove. Gus and I hung over the side of the couch, seeing what would happen next. The three of them were in a circle by the opened door.

"I think I should leave," Harvey said. "Thanks for the delicious pizza."

"No, thank *you!*" Shepherd shouted. "I couldn't have done the job without you."

"You'll have to come back very soon," my mother told Harvey.

"Okay, when?" Harvey asked. He blew his nose on a handkerchief from his jeans pocket. "I'm free most nights and some afternoons."

"Soon," my mother said quickly.

"How about Thanksgiving?" Shepherd asked. "Are you free then?"

"Yes, I am," Harvey said, showing all of his perfect white teeth. It was the first time I had ever seen him smile. "Thanksgiving would be fine."

"Oh, no." My mother shook her head back and forth. "Thanksgiving won't work at all."

"Sure it will, sweetheart," Shepherd said. "We were planning a family dinner. And Harvey, well, you're like family to me!"

"I think I may be your cousin," Harvey said. "I've often thought that."

Shepherd grinned and threw his arm over Harvey's giant shoulders. "Well, then, it's settled. We'll see you on Thursday at four. Right, kids?"

Gus said, "Yes."

"Here?" My mother sounded mad. "You're saying Thursday at four here?"

"I'll bring a dish to pass," Harvey added when he was on the porch.

"Bring that girlfriend of yours, too!" Shepherd shouted outside. "Bring anyone you want! Anyone!"

When Harvey was gone, our mother didn't speak. She looked from the piano, which was in the middle of the hall, back to Shepherd, and then at the shut front door. On TV, the police were chasing the bad guy down twisting streets, and the siren of their car was the only noise. I walked over and turned it off. Then Shepherd pulled a chair from the dining room and sat down at the piano. He began to play.

"Doesn't anyone see what's going on here?" our mother asked all of us when Shepherd had finished his first song.

No one answered.

"Cupcake," Shepherd said, leaning toward the place where our mother was standing.

"Sometimes I can't believe . . . ," she began.

"Sometimes you can't believe how well things work out," Shepherd sang over the music. "I think that's what you're trying to say."

"W"ill you marry me?" Shepherd asked later.

Gus and I were upstairs, brushing our teeth. We went to the banister to listen.

"Thanks for the piano," our mother said. "It was such a . . ."

Gus took his toothbrush out of his mouth and made a gargling noise.

"Such a gesture," our mother said.

"Will you marry me?" Shepherd repeated.

"How many times have you asked me that question?"

"Ten to twelve times," Shepherd's voice said, and I imagined his opened hand, Shepherd counting his own fingers. "That's my best estimate."

Our mother cleared her throat. "And how many times have I said no?"

"Eleven. Not counting this one."

I elbowed Gus in the ribs.

"Good night," our mother said.

"See, I'm waiting for a different answer," Shepherd told her. "One that doesn't have the words *no, good-bye, good night,* or *so long* in it. I guess I'll just keep checking."

"I guess you will," our mother sighed.

The next day was Tuesday and our mother picked us up from school. We drove to Woolworth's, where she said they had pets. She was gripping the steering wheel hard and muttering to herself. I thought it probably had to do with Harvey Kewaygo and his girlfriend coming for Thanksgiving dinner and Shepherd asking her to marry him twelve times. Gus sat slumped in the backseat and whined all the way down State Street because we all knew there were no dogs for sale at the dime store. "I don't want a turtle and I don't want a hamster," he told my mother when we stopped at a stoplight. "And I don't want a goldfish and I do not want a hermit crab."

"You can't be sure of that," my mother said, watching him in the rearview mirror. "You've just convinced yourself that you want a dog, when in fact what you really may want is a turtle. I was reading something in the bookstore just this morning that said some turtles live sixty years. Now that's a pet you could have and enjoy for nearly your whole life."

Even as she was saying it, you could hear how wrong it sounded. Gus went on fake crying. While we were still stopped at the stoplight, I sank down by the window when a boy from my class walked in front of our car.

"What's this about?" my mother asked, eyeing me. "You shouldn't contort yourself. It's very bad for your spine." She tapped her fingernails on the dashboard. "Oh, God. I try so hard and look what happens. I end up having to roast a turkey for a bunch of strangers. And what am I going to do with that monstrosity sitting in the hall? Did you ever know a piano could be so ugly?"

"No," I told her truthfully, peeking out the window.

"Maybe I could get a big tablecloth and keep it covered at all times." She pulled at her coat collar.

"Maybe," I said, sitting up again when we had started to move. "It might work."

"It's a start," she said.

In the dime store, Gus and I wandered to the pet aisle while our mother went to look for a giant tarp or a very big sheet.

"This is terrible," Gus said, when we got to the animal section. We stared at the boxes of catnip and the parrot chewsticks. There were water bowls and rawhide bones. There was even a plaid cushion in a wicker pet bed.

"Here's a dog collar," I said, pointing to one that was red with a silver clasp. "But no dog."

Gus wiped his face on his sleeve. When we had turned around and were watching the guppies and angelfish swimming in their tanks, I felt someone come up and stand close beside me. It was Susie Medicinehat, our old housekeeper. She was holding a laundry basket and a bag of cotton balls and was looking us up and down.

"You've grown a lot," she said after a second. "Both of you."

We hadn't seen her for months and it scared me to see her now, standing in Woolworth's under the bright lights, just like any other person shopping for pot holders or Scotch tape. She didn't fit there at all, with her long shimmering hair and her dark eyes that could stare right through you. I couldn't think of what to say, so I tried to smile.

"You're getting a pet," she told us, jabbing her chin at the tanks of cloudy water. "But don't get a fish."

"I'm not going to," Gus said. "I hope I'm not."

"Get a bird." Susie pointed with her cotton balls to the dirty silver cages off to the right. The three of us stared at the parakeets stretching and screeching behind the thin metal bars. Some of them were white with blue heads. Others were yellow with green wings. One was pinkish-orange with a brown beak. All of them were the colors of Popsicles or Magic Markers, colors that seemed not quite real.

"Get a bird," Susie said again. "A bird is good company. And a bird won't let you down."

"I'm getting a dog," Gus said. "A dog named Roger."

"Hmmm." Susie gave him a long look. "No, I don't see you with any Roger. I see you with a parakeet." She glanced around the store.

Gus ignored her and crouched on the floor to knock on the glass protecting the guinea pigs. A woman came slowly down the aisle pushing a cart and humming something. It sounded like one of the songs Shepherd had played for us on the piano the night before. The woman pushed her cart right down the middle, so I had to step away from Susie as the woman went between us. For a second I could see Susie looking at me as she waited still and quiet while the colored birds flapped their wings in the cages behind her head. She blinked her eyes once under the fluorescent lights as if she had seen the thing she was trying to find. When the woman had passed, Susie stood beside me again.

"Where's your mother?" she asked. Her voice was softer now.

"Over buying a big sheet." I pointed to the far end of the store.

Susie shifted her laundry basket to the other hip. "How is she doing?"

I shoved my hands in my pockets. "She's fine," I said. "She's the same but better."

Susie closed her eyes, thinking. "And you have changed."

She told me this the way you say B comes after A, the way you tell someone the earth is round. "I know," I said, even though I didn't.

She smiled at me and nodded, very slowly. "It's good to see you kids."

Susie began to walk away. I reached out and touched the silky sleeve of her baseball jacket. "I was wondering if you might want to come to our house for Thanksgiving dinner."

Susie turned and raised her eyebrows. "That's a nice offer," she said. "But I do have plans."

"You could come with your husband. We're having lots of people."

"Harvey Kewaygo is bringing his girlfriend," Gus said. He had finished knocking at the guinea pigs and was standing on his tiptoes, choosing a dog collar.

"Well, that's nice of you to invite me," Susie told us, backing away. "I hope you have a real nice time, but like I said, I have other plans. Take care now."

"Maybe you'll decide to come anyway," I said, but Susie had disappeared around a display of plastic plants and couldn't hear me. In their cages the parakeets were chirping all at once.

"I'm getting this." Gus held up a blue collar.

"You probably aren't," I told him.

We left the pet aisle and went and stood in the candy section until our mother came to find us. "What did you decide?" she asked Gus.

He held up the dog collar and a Clark bar. Our mother let out a long breath and loosened her hold on the flowered tablecloth she was carrying folded against her chest.

"A puppy is the only thing I want in the entire world. I won't ever want anything else," he said.

"Think about this," my mother told him. "Once you get a dog, you can't change your mind next week. Or next month. Or next year. He's going to be yours. Permanently."

"Good." Gus grinned.

In the checkout line, while our mother paid for the dog collar and the candy and the tablecloth, I looked for Susie, but she was gone. Outside, she wasn't in the parking lot or walking on the street.

"Please stop," my mother told me when we were back in the car and I had gotten up on my knees on the seat to get a better view. "What is it you're looking for anyway?"

"Susie Medicinehat." I sat flat again and stared straight ahead. "I saw her in the store and I asked her if she wanted to come to our house for Thanksgiving dinner."

My mother put her forehead on the steering wheel and muttered things.

"She said no," I told my mother. "But I think she might change her mind."

"It's snowing!" Gus shouted. He was in the backseat adjusting his new dog collar to different sizes.

My mother sat up and we all pressed our faces to the windows. There was nothing falling from the gray sky except a gum wrapper that had gotten caught in the wind. It came down and brushed our windshield once and blew away.

"It was snowing a minute ago," Gus told us. "You just weren't paying attention."

"You're such a liar," I said.

"Hey." Our mother held up both hands. "I'm calling a little meeting. Now, while it's very thoughtful of you, Annie, to want to include Susie in our dinner, I will ask you to please check with me before you invite others who are not in our immediate family."

"Susie is like family to me," I said.

"Immediate," Gus repeated.

"You don't even know what that means." I turned my face to the cold glass.

"Annie, no arguing, please. I'm already quite agitated." My mother started the car and adjusted the heat vents. She pointed at Gus in the rearview mirror. "And you need to behave yourself if you want to be a pet owner."

"I am behaving," Gus said.

We drove out of the parking lot and down the street in silence. I cupped my breath to the window and wrote my initials and a heart. Then I smeared it all with my knuckles. No one talked until we passed a sign nailed to a tree in someone's front yard that read FREE PAPPIES. Gus started screaming to stop.

"That certainly isn't what you want," my mother told him, not even slowing down or turning around to see.

"Free puppies! Free puppies!" Gus yelled.

"Free pappies," I told him, smiling. "I saw it."

"They meant 'puppies'!" Gus cried, leaning over my mother's shoulder and grabbing at her elbow. "You could tell."

"It's very possible, even probable," my mother said, trying to guide the car down Lake Street. "But I'm not taking any chances at this point. We're talking about people who would put an 'a' instead of a 'u'. That's what concerns me. And I've already got enough I'm worried about."

"They meant 'puppies' and they were free," Gus sniffed. "A whole dog for free!"

"I'm warning you," my mother said to the rearview mirror, but when Gus kept on she shook her head and steered the car to the side of the road. We sat still as a pickup truck roared past us. I knew we were waiting for something more than for Gus to stop crying, but I couldn't say what it was. My mother had forgotten to shut off the turn signal and now it made a clicking noise every few seconds, like someone popping his tongue against the roof of his mouth. She stared down at her hands clasped in her lap. "Ask me," she said.

I turned and looked at Gus, who had quit crying and was holding the loose end of the dog collar, which he'd fastened tight around one of his skinny wrists. He opened his mouth halfway and shut it.

"Ask me," our mother said again, letting each word drop hard, like a stone in the water. "Ask me now and we'll start all over."

I watched as another car flew by, kicking up dead leaves that swirled around our windows. "Ask what?"

My mother leaned over to brush the hair out of my eyes. "Anything."

"Okay," Gus said. "May I please have a dog?"

"Yes, you may. And you know that. So knowing that you will soon get a dog, the right dog, please try to be calm and gracious in the meantime." My mother pulled one of her gloves off her hand and reached into the backseat to shake with Gus. "There, it's a deal."

The three of us kept sitting, letting every car swerve around us.

"Ask me, Annie." My mother wrapped her warm fingers over my cold ones. "Something you would like and I will try."

"Anything?" I bit the inside of my cheek.

"Well, so to speak," my mother said. "Anything."

"I don't know," I told her. I thought of watching TV with Harvey Kewaygo. I thought of standing close to Susie Medicinehat in the dime store. "I'd like a really big family," I said.

"So then," my mother began, sliding her hands back on the steering wheel, "how about if we say that you can invite anyone you want for Thanksgiving dinner. How does that sound?"

"That's not what I meant." I stared out the foggy glass.

My mother reached up and turned off the turn signal. "I know it's not what you meant, but it's a start. And that's what we need here."

"Okay," I said finally.

"I'm happy now," our mother told us, pulling back onto the road when the coast was clear. "I feel good about the way things are going."

"I thought you were upset," I said.

My mother lifted both hands in the air and waved them as if shoving something away. She let the steering wheel float loose, and for a second, no one was driving. "I've changed my mind about all of that," she said after she'd put her hands back.

When we were on our street, I could see Shepherd's truck waiting for us in the driveway.

"But this," she whispered.

"What?" I asked.

"I'm speaking to myself," my mother told me. "People do that sometimes."

That night, Shepherd pushed the piano against a wall in the living room. Earlier, my mother had put the new flowered tablecloth on a high shelf in the closet without ever even taking it out of the bag. Now she and Shepherd stood holding hands, staring at the huge, ugly piano without talking. I sat on the couch doing my math homework while Gus lay on the floor, guessing every answer wrong. When I was working on my fourth division problem, I started to hear sniffling.

"What is it?" my mother asked, stepping back from Shepherd and dropping his hand.

"It's just that this is exactly how I pictured it," he said, his voice cracking.

Gus got up and ran into the other room. When he came back, he was carrying a box of Kleenex and he lifted it up for Shepherd to take one. Shepherd blew his nose and twisted the tissue between his thumbs. "It's like that thing that happens when you know you've seen something before and then when it actually happens it just knocks you over." Shepherd looked at the ceiling. "What is that called?"

"Déjà vu," my mother said.

"Right." Shepherd nodded. "This is like déjà vu. And now it's happening again."

"That's really nice," my mother told him, glancing at Gus and me. "That's good."

"It's more than good!" Shepherd shouted, gripping my mother's shoulders. "It's the best thing ever."

"Maybe not *ever*, Shepherd." My mother patted one of his hands and then brushed it off.

"Ever." Shepherd did a turn in the middle of the carpet and spread his fingers toward the dark windows, the yellow light on the side table, the empty fireplace. "I mean, look at us. Here we are."

"That's true. We're here." My mother held Shepherd's hand again. "But can we talk in the kitchen?"

When Shepherd and my mother had gone down the hall, Gus went and sat on the piano bench and pretended to play a song.

"Cut it out," I said, shutting my math book on my pencil. "You don't know what you're doing."

"You don't." Gus kept banging on the keyboard and when I walked over to make him stop and bent to grab his arm, the light from the lamp in the corner caught the shiny wood just so and I saw the hundreds of numbers invisibly carved into the piano. I had forgotten they were there. I turned my head and they disappeared; I turned it again and they flashed for a second. I pushed in next to Gus and ran my fingers over the tiny lines. Some of them had names written above them and some of them had nothing. There were more than I could count.

Shepherd and my mother were still talking in the kitchen when I went into the hall and dragged the phone on its long cord back to the piano. I crouched and leaned against the piano's cool, dark side and dialed the first number I pointed to. Gus watched, his eyes squinting at me. One number rang and rang twenty times with no one answering. The next one said that the phone was out of order. Then, on the third try, from a number carved near the very bottom edge, a woman said hello. I covered the mouthpiece with my palm. Gus was playing the same note over and over and I could feel the sound through my back. "Who is this?" the woman asked, her voice tiny and far away. "Who's there?"

After I'd hung up, my heart was beating all the way through my sweater. Outside, a gust of wind rattled the screens.

"What are you doing?" Gus stared down at me.

"Nothing," I told him. I put my face close to the piano and dialed again, fast, a number written under the word *June.*

"Yeah?" It was a man's voice, scratchy and deep.

"June," I said, uncovering the mouthpiece.

"Just a second." The phone on the other end hit something hard and I could hear the hissing of the wind over the wires. Then I could hear someone's footsteps coming toward me.

"Yes?" a voice asked. "Hello?" It sounded exactly like Mrs. Babcock, the school nurse. Mrs. Babcock had blond curly hair, and once she had let me lie down on the white cot in the sick room for two whole hours, just because I was having a bad day. She had told me that everything would be all right if I shut my eyes for a while, and she had put her hand on my forehead and kept it there. That was how this voice sounded.

"Hello?" the woman said.

"Hi." I traced my finger along a pattern on the Oriental rug. "Hi."

"Hi, yourself. Who is this?"

"Annie." My own name felt strange in my mouth.

"Annie!" The beautiful voice laughed. "God, I didn't know you were in town! When did you get in?"

"I've been here," I said. Then it was quiet and I could hear the hissing again.

"Wait a minute, who is this?"

"Annie." No one said anything for a second.

"Annie from the lounge, right?"

In the background the man shouted, "Just hang up if it's that smart-ass Ricky again!"

I could hear the woman breathing softly.

"Annie from Pepe's Lounge, right?"

I sneezed.

"Bless you," the beautiful voice said. "Now, look, I'm trying to work here. Who is this?"

"This is Annie and I'm calling . . ." I stared up at the ceiling, the way Shepherd did when he was trying to think of a certain word. "I'm calling because . . ."

"Because we wanted to know if you wanted to come over on Thanksgiving!" Gus yelled. I leaned over and tried to swat him, but he jumped to the side and the phone cord wouldn't reach.

There was a long sigh on the phone. "Hey, Annie or whoever you are, I don't know what kind of prank this is, but I'm pretty busy right now and I sure don't appreciate the interruption."

"I'm sorry," I said.

"You should be." I could hear the woman take a puff on a cigarette and blow smoke right into my ear. "You know how hard it is to earn a living?"

I picked a spot of chipped paint on the ceiling to stare at and held my breath. "You could come over for Thanksgiving," I said. "If you wanted to."

"Well, that's in two days! Of course I've got plans. So, no thanks, I guess."

Gus had stopped pretending to play the piano and was leaping around the room, dodging close but out of reach.

"Okay," I said, tucking my knees to my chest and balancing the phone tight in the curve of my neck. "But maybe you'll change your mind."

"Come on over!" Gus yelled from where he was bouncing on the couch.

"Here's my advice," the beautiful voice whispered. "You sound really, really, really young and if I were you, I'd stop whatever I was doing and give it a rest because none of us has much time to just enjoy, you know? Be young when you're young."

I watched Gus hopping up and down on the furniture with his arms waving in the air. "Okay," I said. "I will."

"You do that."

There was a dial tone, but I still held the phone to my ear, not wanting to put it down. Shepherd stuck his head around the doorway. "Pssst," he said to Gus. "How about if I take you ice fishing tomorrow? If your mom says it's okay with her?"

"Annie's calling people from the piano," Gus told him.

"Gotcha." Shepherd put one finger to his lips. "I'll be quiet."

"No, I mean she's inviting them over to our house for Thanksgiving dinner," Gus said.

"Oh, that's a very great idea. I've invited a bunch of friends, too." Shepherd smiled. "Now don't forget, ice fishing tomorrow. You and me, amigo. Two men and their fishing poles." He pointed at Gus and disappeared down the hall.

"The lake isn't even frozen," I said. "There isn't any ice."

Gus lifted his shoulders and tilted his head to one side. "Are those people coming over for Thanksgiving?" he asked.

"Maybe." I hung up the phone but stayed crouched on the floor next to the silent piano.

"I'm going ice fishing and I'm getting a dog." Gus sat back on the couch and shut his eyes. He folded his small hands over his stomach. "I'm happy now."

I pressed one side of my face hard to the piano's cool wood. I felt the phone numbers on my skin, their tiny grooves and loops cutting against my cheek. I listened to Shepherd's and my mother's voices, echoing softly from the other room. "What if no one comes over?" I asked, too low for Gus to hear, but he did anyway.

"There will be one hundred people and they will all have fun and maybe move in," Gus said, not opening his eyes. "I know. And also, Shepherd is going to live here."

"I doubt it," I told him.

"You'll see," Gus said. His eyes were still shut and there were purple shadows the shape of half-moons falling across his forehead. "I know that it's true."

Shepherd was scraping frost off his truck windshield at seven o'clock the next morning. It was barely light out, but I could see the brown trees with no leaves, the silver-coated street with no tire tracks, all of it still and quiet except for Shepherd. I watched him from my bedroom window, standing in front of the closed curtains in my nightgown. When he looked up and saw me, he waved. He said something, cupping his hand to his mouth, but I couldn't hear what it was. He kissed his fingers and reached toward me.

After he'd driven away, I went downstairs, past Gus's room, where he was still lying in a lump under his blankets. My mother was sitting at the kitchen table, holding a coffee cup and writing on a pad of paper. The room smelled like cinnamon toast and there were two plates with burned crumbs and two crumpled napkins next to her elbow.

"Sit down," she told me, pulling out the chair next to hers. "Tell me how this sounds: turkey, stuffing, sweet potatoes, regular potatoes, green beans, cranberry sauce, rolls, pumpkin pie, and apple pie. I thought it would be nice to have something for those people who don't like pumpkin pie, like me for instance." She took a sip of coffee. "What do you think?"

"It's okay." I kicked my slippers on a chair rung and picked at one of the crumpled napkins, the one I thought Shepherd had probably used.

"Just okay?" My mother wrinkled her eyebrows together. "I thought it sounded basically flawless." She held her cup in the air and studied me. The sun was coming up now and I watched a thin icicle hanging under the outside eaves drip once. My mother pushed her chair back and took my hand. "Come in here for a second," she said, leading me into the living room and over to the ugly piano.

We sat together side by side on the narrow, splintered bench. My mother began to play. It was music like something you could only invent in your head, music from some kind of dream. She played for a long time, not even looking at the keys, her hair drifting loose around her shoulders. When she started something faster, her whole body moved along the piano. Then she took my hands and had me lay them, one, then the other, over her own. We played a song like that, together, our hands stretching slowly up and down, up and down the chipped white keyboard, our fingers laced tight. We were laughing when she lifted our hands and stopped.

"I didn't know you could play," I told her.

"I didn't, either." She reached for her coffee cup, which she'd set on top of the piano, near the painting of the moose.

"I mean, I'd forgotten." She traced her fingernail over the names etched in the wood, all of the hearts and numbers written there. "Sometimes I think I've forgotten more things than I'll ever be able to remember." She hit one key. "Like this."

"Did you take lessons?" I asked her. "To learn to play?"

She smoothed her hair behind her ears. "For a couple of years," she said. "Starting when I was about your age. But your aunt Claire was always so much better than I was, and I guess I got tired of it, all the practicing. So after a while, I just quit. Until right now."

"I'd like to take lessons."

"Okay." She turned and smiled at me. "You can do that." She looked at her watch. "It's already seven thirty."

"Why did you remember you could play the piano today and not yesterday?"

She shrugged and took a sip of coffee. "Because today I wanted to remember." She stood and started walking toward the kitchen. "You'd better go and get dressed now and wake Gus. I'll drive you to school and then when I pick you up, we can go to the grocery and get all of the food for our big turkey dinner."

"Have I forgotten things?" I stayed sitting on the piano bench, watching her disappearing back.

"Oh, of course. Everyone does," she called. "But not like I have. So it's not something to even think about. Go get ready, okay?"

On the way to school we passed the yard with the FREE PAPPIES sign nailed to the tree trunk. We all turned to look. Someone had crossed out the "a" with a line and put a big black "u" in its place.

"I said so," Gus told us. "I knew."

"What did we decide yesterday, Gus?" My mother glanced at him.

"I am behaving," he said. "I do want to own a pet."

That afternoon, after school and the grocery store, Shepherd came in his truck to take Gus fishing in the Sturgeon River. He had brought a smaller-sized fishing pole for Gus to use, and he had packed a thermos of hot chocolate and oatmeal cookies in a little knapsack that Gus had already strapped on over his jacket.

"You will stay on shore," my mother told Shepherd before they left.

"Why wouldn't we?" Shepherd laughed. He was tying a red muffler around Gus's neck and helping him with his mittens.

"Because last night you used the term 'ice fishing,'" my mother reminded him.

"That's just a figure of speech," Shepherd said. "I only meant that it was going to be pretty chilly. I like to pretend there's ice. I like to imagine there's snow. It makes it more exciting that way."

Shepherd kneeled to whisper in my ear. When he leaned close, I could see all the tiny crinkles around his eyes. "Annie, I don't want you to feel left out," he said. "I'm planning something for us to do, too, okay? Something that you'd like."

He patted Gus on the knapsack and growled. "All set, buddy? Two men off to struggle against the elements and return the victors."

My mother stood on the front porch in her stocking feet. "Please be careful."

"Okay, Mom. We'll be careful." Shepherd winked at her. He bent to kiss her cheek and she tilted it up to meet him.

When they had gone, I helped my mother take the groceries from the paper sacks lining the kitchen counters and fill the cupboards and refrigerator. My mother talked about how she would fix each dish, about how she would get up at five A.M. to start the turkey. "There'll be how many of us?" she asked as she was sorting the cans of pumpkin and condensed milk into a little group. "You're in charge of that."

I counted in my head. "Twenty," I told her. "Maybe thirty."

"What?" She held a bunch of parsley in the air.

"Well, I invited my teacher, Mrs. Birdsall, and a lady on the phone, and Susie Medicinehat and her husband, and Shepherd invited some friends, and then there's Aunt Claire, and Harvey Kewaygo and his girlfriend, and Gus and . . ."

"I get the picture," my mother said, putting her palm on her forehead. "No need to continue."

"There are a lot of people, but they might not all come," I said.

I folded one of the paper bags, and when I looked over, my mother was standing by the sink with her wrists held under the running water. She was staring out at the lawn, at the empty trees and the flat, shining lake, and she was crying. I touched her elbow, but she didn't look at me.

"This isn't because I'm sad," she said to the window. "This is because I'm happy."

We didn't say anything else for what seemed like a long time. I listened to the hissing radiator and noticed the half-opened cupboards, the squatty cans and rounded jars, the way my mother had placed them, so carefully, all in their rows. "It's like what Shepherd was talking about," I told her. "That thing that happens when you picture something and then it's there."

"It's something like that." My mother rubbed her knuckles over her cheeks. She turned off the faucet and dried her hands on a dish towel. "I hope everyone does come for Thanksgiving," she told me after a minute. "But even if they don't, we'll still have a great time."

I nodded.

"Do you like Shepherd?" my mother asked.

I pushed a can of condensed milk back and forth on the counter with one finger. "He's really nice."

"Okay." My mother nodded her head yes. I could tell it was the answer she had wanted to hear.

"Will you help me make an apple pie?" she asked. By then her eyes were perfectly clear, as if she hadn't been crying at all.

The puppy Shepherd and Gus brought back from fishing a while later was white with black spots. "We had to," Shepherd explained to my mother. "We didn't catch a thing, not one fish, and then we passed this house that had a sign right in the front yard for free dogs. So you can imagine. We had to stop."

"Roger!" Gus called to the dog when it ran into the next room and came out with one of our mother's shoes in its mouth.

"Very bad boy!" Shepherd yelled, but he sounded happy as he said it.

"This is going to be your responsibility," my mother told Gus. "You're going to have to feed him, and take him for walks, and make sure that he doesn't chew up our shoes."

We were all in the living room, watching Roger run in circles near the coffee table. The whole house smelled like the pie that was baking in the oven. Shepherd cracked his knuckles and sat down to play the piano. Roger bit the cuff of his jeans leg and pulled with his tiny, pointy teeth. I lay on my back on the rug near Shepherd's feet, letting Roger nip at my hair. My mother was off to the side, pretending to read a magazine and watching us.

"It's snowing!" Gus shouted, and everyone except Shepherd went to the window to see. Outside, there was only the same blank sky.

"You know better than to fib," my mother said, after she'd knelt on the couch to look past the curtains, up at the low clouds.

"It's snowing somewhere," Gus told her.

"I'm sorry," Shepherd said over the music. "I'm afraid he got that one from me."

"I got that from Shepherd," Gus agreed, bending to pet the fur on Roger's head and sneak him the broken half of an oatmeal cookie.

"No more lying," my mother said.

"It's not a lie if you want it to be true," Shepherd sang. *"So darling, please just let me take care of you."*

"What do you think?" Shepherd looked over his shoulder at my mother.

"Catchy." She smiled with only her mouth.

"I wrote it just now!" Shepherd shouted as he banged on the keyboard. "And I meant every word!"

"That's what worries me sometimes," my mother said, too softly for Shepherd to hear.

"That's the beauty of it!" he yelled a minute later, singing to the ceiling. "You know, darling-darling, that's the very best part."

.   .   .

S hepherd's truck was in the driveway at eleven thirty when I woke up and went to look outside. There were no street-lights on our street, but the moon lit the edges of everything, catching the whip of the radio antenna, one door handle, a hubcap. I blew my breath against the glass and it all went fuzzy and blurred. Then, after a second, it was clear again and Shepherd's truck was still there in the dark, waiting.

O n Thanksgiving our mother cooked all morning, using every pot and pan we owned and what seemed like every dish from every cupboard. She moved around the kitchen hum-ming and banging the oven door open and closed, laughing even when something spilled or when she dropped her good serving bowl. "We should have done this a long time ago," she told me, as I held the dustpan and she swept up the broken pieces of the bowl and dumped them into the trash. "Had a big party, I mean."

At noon Shepherd helped her put the extra leaf in the din-ing room table and they dragged chairs from every part of the house. There was enough room for eighteen people, and I set each place carefully with the heavy silver forks and knives, the creamy white napkins, the miniature salt and pepper shakers. When I was through, I stared at my ghost reflection in one of the plates my mother had rubbed shiny with a linen cloth.

"Don't worry, you're pretty much perfect," Shepherd told me.

He was leaning in the doorway, chewing on one of the radish roses my mother had made to decorate the hors d'oeuvre tray. My mother had gone upstairs to clean up and put on different clothes, and Gus was in the front yard, throwing a ball for Roger to chase.

"I just wondered if I could see myself in this, that's all," I said. I put the plate down and picked at one of the tulips drooping from the big vase in the center of the table.

Shepherd finished eating his rose. He smoothed his hands together, as if brushing away crumbs. "Hey, promise me something," he said, still leaning in the doorway.

"Maybe." I held the top of one of the straight-backed chairs and tapped my knee on the middle rung.

Shepherd smiled slowly. He took his thumbs and first fingers and made them into a perfect square. He brought his hands to his face and looked at me like that, through his fingers, as if they were a camera and I was the picture. "Don't change too much."

I didn't move. "I already have," I said.

Shepherd shook his head and dropped his hands. He looked out the window. Gus was lying on his back on the brown grass while Roger leapt on his stomach, barking. The red ball held high in Gus's hand was the only color in the afternoon. "Then stay," Shepherd said, "just about like you are right now."

People starting knocking on the door at three thirty and by four o'clock there were fifteen of them sitting in the living room, drinking wine and listening to Shepherd bang on the piano. Four more were standing in the hallway and kitchen.

"Who are they all?" my mother whispered to me. "I only

know Margaret from the bookstore." She was leaning over the open oven, basting the turkey. She had an apron tied over her blue silk dress, but she'd already spilled something dark near her collar.

"I only know three of them," I said, handing her a hot pad. "Aunt Claire, Gus, and Shepherd."

"This is a delicious shrimp puff, Paige," one of the men by the sink said. He wiped his mouth with a paper towel and smiled.

"Really great," the woman with curly hair next to him agreed. "And that turkey looks completely yummy."

My mother looked at me. "That's the doorbell again," she said in a soft voice. "Annie, will you go answer it, please?"

When I squeezed past the crowd in the hall, Harvey Kewaygo had already let himself in. He was carrying a green Jell-O mold on a platter covered with plastic wrap. He handed Gus his jacket and gave me the plate of Jell-O. "I made this myself," Harvey said, showing his straight, shiny teeth. "Now I'd like you to meet my girlfriend," he told us. "This is Grace Nanagost."

"Hi, Grace," Gus said.

"Jesus, I haven't seen you two for a while," Grace muttered, frowning. "Or your mother for that matter."

"You all are acquainted?" Harvey asked Grace.

"Yeah, yeah." Grace shrugged.

"She was our babysitter," I told Harvey. "But not for quite a while."

Grace pointed her fingernail at me. "Now that all had to do with simple miscommunication." She turned to Harvey and punched him in the shoulder. "You said 'dinner at a friend's house' so when we turned in the driveway here . . . if I'd have known you meant these friends . . ." She looked down at her tight pink blouse. "I'd have dressed up a little more." She threw her poncho toward Gus and punched Harvey's giant shoulder again. "I'm going to go find something to drink."

"So, how've you been?" Harvey asked Gus.

I walked over and put Harvey's Jell-O on the dining room table. Then I went back and poked my head around the corner and peeked into the living room. Most of the people were sitting on the carpet or crowded around the piano, where Shepherd was taking requests for favorite songs. Aunt Claire was by the fireplace, talking to a skinny man I recognized from the post office. Someone had opened all of the windows and Grace was already perched on the sill of one of them, letting the wind blow and tangle her hair as she held a wineglass to her lips.

In the kitchen, my mother was scraping sweet potatoes into a big bowl. "They have vitamin K," the woman with curly hair was telling her. "Were you aware of that?"

"Annie sweetheart, will you call everyone for dinner, please? Dear?" My mother leaned close. "Hurry," she whispered. "This is getting a little out of control."

"Dinner!" I yelled, walking from room to room. "Time for dinner, please!"

"And it's about time," Grace said, not moving from the window.

"Isn't this great?" Shepherd asked when I came past the piano. "There must be at least thirty people here!"

"There aren't enough plates," I told him, watching everyone push toward the dining room. "Or enough chairs."

"Aw, we'll use paper plates. We'll sit on cardboard boxes."
Shepherd took a sip from his drink. "What matters is that they
showed up."

"Who are they?" I watched a tall man place his hand gently
on Aunt Claire's back and guide her across the room.

Shepherd laughed. "Beats me! But I guess I must know
them from somewhere."

"Is this what you had in mind?" my mother asked, coming
to stand beside Shepherd and me as we watched our guests find
places to sit.

"Sort of," I told her. "Maybe not exactly."

"This is exactly what I had in mind," Shepherd said.

When we were all around the table, some people sharing
chairs, other people eating from TV trays or sitting on the carpet, that was what Shepherd told them. "I feel like I know all of
you and I'm just glad you're here," he said, lifting his glass of
wine. "That's my toast."

"And to a fabulous turkey," the man from the post office
said, raising his teacup to my mother. "The best I've ever eaten."

"And to a great time," a woman with a space between her
front teeth added.

Most people nodded and took a sip.

"And Susie Medicinehat," Gus said loudly, pointing outside
to where Susie was standing on the sidewalk. She was staring at
our house, holding something close to her coat.

"Oh, I'm glad!" Shepherd said. "Another guest."

I waved to Susie. "I'll let her in." I got up and went to open
the front door. Susie was on the porch, stamping her boots.

"This is pumpkin," she said, handing me a pie pan. It was still warm against my fingers.

"Come in!" someone shouted from the dining room, but Susie shook her head no.

"Please." I touched her sleeve. "Please stay."

She scowled, but pulled off her hat and followed me into the hall. Shepherd had gotten out of his chair and he took Susie's arm and made her sit in his place. Susie hunched in the chair, not talking. Aunt Claire and three other people were clearing the dinner plates and my mother was putting out smaller ones from the china cabinet for dessert. I got a knife and starting cutting thin slivers of Susie's pie for the lady with curly hair to pass around the table. Everyone was talking at once, but Susie didn't say a word. She just looked out the window, at the lawn and the street, as if that was where she wanted to be.

After the coffee had been poured and all of the pie served, my mother sat down again at her spot at the end of the table. She lifted her empty plate.

"Now how did that happen?" Aunt Claire asked. "We forgot to give you a piece."

The woman with curly hair went to pass my mother a slice of the apple one, holding it out on the silver pie cutter, but my mother moved her plate away, quick, with a jerk of her wrist. She was staring at Susie. "I should tell you," my mother said, pronouncing every word carefully. "Thank you for saving my life."

All around the table, everyone stopped eating.

"To whom are you referring?" Aunt Claire asked my

mother. She took a sip of coffee and pretended to laugh, as if what my mother had said was a joke. A few other people laughed, too, but then they quit. Everything was silent except for Gus tapping his fork on the rim of his milk glass.

"Thanks for saving my life," my mother said again.

Susie looked down at her lap. "I never saved your life."

"Yes, you did." My mother smiled. "And I'd like to thank you."

Susie shook her head and mumbled something none of us could hear. Aunt Claire held her napkin over her mouth, and Grace Nanagost squinted at my mother from across the room. A man with thick glasses who was eating from one of the TV trays cleared his throat.

"Paige, you've worn yourself out," Aunt Claire told my mother. She turned to the woman beside her. "She's just overly tired," Aunt Claire whispered.

"Oh, I meant it," my mother said. "A few people here have saved my life. Susie is only one of them."

"Cupcake." Shepherd reached over and patted my mother's hand. "We know what you meant."

He pushed back the chair he was sharing with Gus and stood up fast, knocking his big knee against the table. Harvey reached out to catch his wineglass and keep the wine from spilling, but a few drops of dark red splashed over the side.

"Sit back, please," Shepherd told everyone. "Remove your elbows."

"Listen," Susie started to say, but by then Shepherd had grabbed the edge of the tablecloth and yanked it high, pulling it hard and sure with his entire body. For a second, everything hung there, perfect and not moving, the sugar bowl with its rounded lid, the plates of half-eaten pie, the silver teaspoons and crumpled napkins, all of it hung in the air above us. I shut my eyes. When I opened them again, each thing—the vase of flowers, the tiny pitcher of cream, the cups and their saucers, the crystal ashtray—was sitting exactly as it had been before, now on the bare wood of the table, and Shepherd was bowing, wrapped in the long white cloth. I could hear the slow drip of the water faucet in the kitchen.

"I knew he was going to do that," Gus said, taking a drink from his still rippling glass of milk. "I could tell."

Grace Nanagost was the first to clap, but one by one everyone joined in. Harvey whistled and cheered. "Shep," he said, pounding Shepherd on the back. "Good old Shep." The woman with curly hair shrieked and threw her arms around Shepherd's neck. "That's the best trick I've seen!" she yelled. "Ever!"

"Get a camera!" the man from the post office shouted. Aunt Claire picked up her saucer and peered underneath it, then set it back down. Shepherd was laughing and bowing and my mother was watching him, clapping lightly with her fingers held stiff. Her eyes glanced away from Shepherd to something across the room, then to the window. I knew she was already imagining the next thing.

"He really didn't have to do that, did he?" she whispered when I went and crouched beside her chair. She smiled down at me and smoothed my hair. "But I guess it's okay. Everything's okay now."

For a few minutes we all sat or stood, staring at the table. People touched a cup or a fork and shook their heads or laughed. Shepherd shrugged. When Aunt Claire began clearing away the empty glasses, it was as if the spell had been broken and people began to get up and move. "It seems like a shame to touch anything," a woman in a green dress said. "Maybe we should leave it all for a while."

Aunt Claire didn't answer, but kept clearing, and some people took their coffee cups into the living room and sat on the couch or on the carpet around the fire. Other people helped collect the dirty plates and a few people left, clicking the front door quietly behind. One of them was Susie Medicinehat. I saw her out the hall window when she was already too far gone, walking away down the middle of our street. My mother went into the kitchen and Gus let Roger out of the upstairs bedroom where he'd been keeping him during the party. I helped Aunt Claire carry dishes and then, when no one was looking, I put on my coat and went and stood on the back porch, alone in the clear cold.

"Come outside with me," Shepherd said, opening the screen door.

"I am outside." I breathed into my mittens and shuffled my scuffed patent leather shoes on the creaky porch boards.

"No, I mean really outside." Shepherd buttoned his coat and I followed him out onto the lawn. The sky was purple-black and I could hear voices floating from the house. "Everything's just fine," Shepherd told me. "So if you're worrying, don't."

"I'm not," I said.

We listened to the faraway voices, to someone's high laugh, to Roger's barking.

"Ten years from now I'll still be inside there, banging on that piano. Doing stupid magic tricks." Shepherd pointed back over his shoulder. "I think your mother is almost in love with me, and I'm not going anywhere. Not for a long, long time. I can promise you that."

"Okay." I nodded in the dark. It was so cold I was shivering, loose inside my sleeves.

"This is sort of where we are." Shepherd put his arm around me. "This is our home."

I nodded again and felt the heaviness of his warm arm. I didn't know why he was saying those things.

"God, it's beautiful," Shepherd said, staring up. "I always forget how beautiful it is." He turned and took one of my mittens in his bare hand, then the other. "Here," he said, lifting me. "Step onto my feet."

I stood on his work boots and he spun me in a circle.

"See?" he said.

We dipped and swayed until I was dizzy, until the lit windows of the house were watery and blurred.

"Now you're waltzing," he told me.

I put my face to his wool coat. It smelled like smoke and like spilled wine. I held on to Shepherd and he held me back. The frozen lawn crunched like broken glass under Shepherd's boots and the moon was small and gray above his head. I thought of something perfect: the way everything had looked hanging in the air just before it all landed on the table without a sound. I remembered it the way a piece of a dream comes flying back like a bright bird.

Shepherd was humming.

"Now you're dancing," he said. "In case you were wondering."

"We're dancing," I told him. "I know."

Acknowledgments

I owe great thanks to many people, but to two women in particular. Rebecca Strong, my agent, is brilliant and wonderful, an advocate and friend. I feel so lucky to know her. Shaye Areheart is the sort of editor about whom writers dream. I would claim she's psychic, but I think it's more that she is just so incredibly good at what she does. She makes it seem like magic. I admire her so very much and am so happy to call her a friend. Love and gratitude to Rebecca; love and gratitude to Shaye.

Heartfelt thanks to everyone at Shaye Areheart Books and Three Rivers Press who has worked so hard to make this book the best it can be, especially Sibylle Kazeroid, Joshua Poole, Laurie McGee, Jim Gullickson, Selina Cicogna, and Ava Kavyani. Your time and care have made all the difference.

Love and thanks to Jaimy Gordon, for reading from another continent, for being such a good friend to this book. And thanks and love to Stuart Dybek, who was there from the start.

So much love to my family, especially to Gow and Cameron,

for all their continued support. And love and thanks to Seberon and Dianne, Haley, Peter, and Hanna.

And so very much love to my husband, Hank. He believed in this book with his whole and generous heart. Thank you for everything. You are my love, H.

About the Author

LIESEL LITZENBURGER'S first novel, *The Widower*, was published by Shaye Areheart Books in 2006. Her stories and essays have appeared in magazines and anthologies. She has taught writing at several colleges and universities, including the University of Michigan, New College, and the Interlochen Arts Academy, and is the recipient of awards and residencies from the Michigan Council for Arts and Cultural Affairs, Yaddo, and the MacDowell Colony. She lives in Michigan.

Also by Liesel Litzenburger

*What if every life is connected to every other
by a single thread?*

Weaving threads of love and
mystery through every page,
Liesel Litzenburger's spare and
lyrical novel follows the lives
of unforgettable characters in
a profound story of loss and
redemption.

THE WIDOWER
$23.00 ($30.00 Canada)
0-307-33879-7

Available from Shaye Areheart Books wherever books are sold